# GOD'S CHOSEN GANGSTER'S

William Taylor

authorHOUSE®

AuthorHouse™
1663 Liberty Drive
Bloomington, IN 47403
www.authorhouse.com
Phone: 833-262-8899

Published by AuthorHouse 05/27/2021

ISBN: 978-1-6655-2702-6 (sc)
ISBN: 978-1-6655-2700-2 (hc)
ISBN: 978-1-6655-2701-9 (e)

Library of Congress Control Number: 2021910524

Print information available on the last page.

This book is printed on acid-free paper.

# CONTENTS

# PART I

PART 1

# JUST MADE IT HOME

Getting of the boat in San Diego seemed surreal to Timothy Johnson. Pulling into the dock on the U.S.S. Ronald Regan, the first thing he noticed was how many people who had showed up to greet the Marines. They had just finished a year long tour in Iraq. He had been gone so long; the modern buildings and vehicles looked strange to him. Even seeing the people, the women in their sun dresses and sandals, the kids in their shorts and tennis shoes was a sight for sore eyes. He couldn't believe he was finally home. "Man look at all these bitches" he said to his partner who was smiling and taking in the unreal ness of the moment. "Man, do you mean women, those are our comrade's wives, sisters and daughters. Why you wanna come off like that?" Come off like what? Like I'm tired of looking at you stankin mutha Fuckers in these tired ass tan fatigues"? They know we are looking at them, that's why they got dressed like that. You know your lookin at'em too. Look at her! Them can't be real! Tim was looking at a Snow Bunny revealing too much cleavage of some 38 double D's in a green form fittin dress. She was standing with a little boy who had to be about 2 years old. "Well you know she ain't here for you", Jason said, "and you better watch your gaze. You might get your ass kicked out here today. They were trying to be quite because the captain was about to speak.

"As we stand here today, you men, women and children can be proud of your family members, who stand here today as United States marines. They have set out to and succeeded in the mission their country called on them to do. There are no words I can say that could express the full gratitude that is owed these marines today. The jobs you performed was often above and beyond what was expected of you. But then that would imply that you are ordinary people. But you are extra ordinary people. You are United States Marines. The crowd let out a tremendous uproar and clapped as the captain continued. So I'm not going to hold you here to long today, because I know you're anxious to get to your families which some of you have been away from for almost two years. So as you leave here today, know that your family members have made a difference for the citizen of Iraq and the people of that region by helping to form a thriving Democracy so that its people can enjoy some of the freedoms that we have come to hold so dear. With that may Gold Bless you all and God Bless America. "Yeah! Welcome Home" shouts rang out from the crowd as the marines tossed their berets in the air and joined in the applause. Timothy participated in the celebration with a bit of apathy because although he knew the celebration was for him, there'd be no family there to greet him. As he watched the women in the green dress jump up and down, he was in a trance. Then a young marine carrying a duffle bag walked up to her and lifted her in his arms. He came out of his trance when Jason got in his ear and said, "See, he probably has her because he doesn't jump from one woman to the next as soon he sees some pretty round thing shaking in front of him". Ah shut that shit up Nigga. God put women here for us to enjoy and for them to enjoy us. Beside that, I aint trippin on that broad. Nigga we back in the land of Milk and Honies", I'll bet you $500.00 we're gonna have some bitches better than that before the night is over". We in Cali Baby! You mean you're gonna have one better than that, man you know I'm married. Playboy you mean to tell me that after almost 18 months in that desert, them bitches covering their assess and titties, given the chance you wouldn't nail one of these broads to the bed? "Hell nah man, I've been married for five years and I take my marriage serious". "It must not be that serious to her. You've been gone all this time and she isn't even here to greet you. She's probably breaking Tyrone off one more

2

time." "Nigga you worried about the wrong shit", Jason said. I told you she's a police officer and they have a lot of shit going on in Detroit right now. She hasn't had a day off in 2 months because they can't find any qualified recruits." "Um huh. Her and her cock diesel partner is probably putting in more overtime than you think". "Nigga I done told you about disrespecting my wife. You're determined to get your ass kicked out here on this deck, huh?" Jason stood about 6' 3" and he had hands almost half the size of Tim's head. Besides that, he had organized a fight club in Kuwait when they where waiting to be deployed to the front lines. He had made a lot of money from fools who took his subtleness as a weakness.

Tim took that opportunity to change the subject. "Nah nigga you know I'm just playin. You know her better than me. This mutha fucka is always so serious." "well what you want to do man?' he had noticed that the Marines who had family meet them where starting to leave the dock area. "Shit I wasn't really feelin staying in the barracks tonight. We only got 24 hours to chill," Jason said, "we might as well go get pressed and hit the town. To see how these dudes really get down out here. They where issued commercial flight tickets to return to their home towns. Tim had a one way ticket for Denver, where Jason had a layover until he boarded a flight to Detroit. They where scheduled to fly out of LAX the next day at noon. With their commitment to the marines filled they were now regular citizens. Ay that's what I'm talking about, we can take the charter bus up to LA so if we get too fucked up tonight we won't miss our flight. Besides that I know some poppin ass spots in Santa Monica we can hit and we can get some gear. "Yeah man I'm with that. As long as we're not around any of those ignorant niggas and that bullshit", Jason said. "Man you always sound like that nigga "Rese" off Menace to Society. You know it's gone be ignorant mutha fuckers where ever you go. As long as you don't say nothing to them, they ain't gone say nothing to you." I hope you right man let's go ahead and get this bus before we have to wait another hour.

Before they got to their rooms, they made a pit stop at the Beverly

Center. "Shit, I got to get clean. I'm gonna be so glad to get the fuck out of these fatigues", Tim said. What do you think I should get? "You should get you one of those zebra striped jockey drawers and a tank top. Then go down Santa Monica Boulevard to see what you can catch", Jason said laughing. Man I ain't worried about you; I've got to get my own shit. For sure than nigga, I'll meet you at the hotel at 2 o'clock. We're gonna be at the Best Western on Oceanview Parkway. Yeah, dismissed soldier.

Just as Tim was going threw the Designer clothes displays, one of the sales reps approached him. She said, "Can I help you find something today?" Tim hadn't noticed her at first but when he looked up, he was at a loss for words. She was about 5'8", smooth dark brown skin. Her hair was black and silky. Cut short in the front but long in the back. She had an oval face, like Naomi Campbells, with dark brown Chinese eyes. Her low cut, form fitting blouse could barely hold what Tim referred to as her big boy toys. Her waist was thin and her pants were only loose enough so you could tell it wasn't her skin.

"No ma'am, Tim said, "I'm just searching for a couple of outfits so I can blend in with the natives." "Well, that's what I'm here for, and don't call me ma'am, I'm only 23 years old. "Oh, that's just out of habit, I didn't intend to offend you. What would you prefer I call you?" Tim asked. She poked her chest out then pointed to her name tag, she said, "my name is Tia and what's yours?" he said, "I'm Tim". She said "you're not from here?" No, no, I'm not but how did you know that? Tia said, "Cause the dudes around here don't talk like that plus you said you're trying to blend in with the natives. Yeah, I did say that, huh. I just came back from over sea's and I'll only be here for a short while before I head back home. Umh. And where is home? I'm from a city just outside of Denver. It's been a long time since I've been home. My unit just came back from Iraq today and this is my first time in Cali, so I wanted to see if everything they say about this town is true. Well what do they say? From what I hear, they say that you haven't done nothing until you've done it in Cali. "That's true", Tia said, "that's true, you might mess around and fall in love. Then you'll never see your wife and kids again. "Yeah that's what I'm talking about, but I don't have any wife or kids. I only have my brother waiting on me, Tim said. You trying to tell me a nice looking brother like you, don't have a woman?

Tim stood at 6'1". He was fair complicated and had light brown eyes. He wore his hair in a Taper fade, and was very muscular built. He said, "Nah, I've been gone for awhile and the friend I had, told me that her flesh could get weak and she didn't wanna make any promises. Oh, I'm sorry to hear that. Then you definitely got to get your party on. What do you plan on doing? You know I don't know. Me and my partner is probably going to heave a drink or two somewhere. Could you give my any suggestions?" She said, "How about call me later and I'll see what's poppin tonight". Ay that sounds like a good idea. Are you going to be able to escort us? "Will see", Tia said, "let's go ahead and get you something to wear so you don't look like a tourist".

# BACK TO THE HOTEL

As Tim was getting out of the cab at the Best Western he thought, yeah it's well after 2 o'clock. This dude should already have us checked in. But when he asked for Jason Hephners room number, the clerk said no one under that name was staying there. He said "Damm, I hope this dude didn't get lost". The clerk said, "I'm sorry sir?" Oh nothing Ma'am, I'm just thinking out loud. I need a room with double occupancy. She said "for how long?' he said, "just for tonight". She said "the room will be $175, check out is at eleven, you can feel-free to use the pool, weight room and we have free movies. There was a complimentary breakfast and room service until midnight. She said "will that be cash or credit?" He said credit. She said "thank you sir. You'll be in room 227 and would you like a bell hop to assist you with your bags? He said, "No ma'm, I'll be fine, thank you. She said ok, thanks for choosing to stay with us and if you need anything give us a call to the front desk.

Tim was just ready to relax. It had been along time since he really had a chance to stretch-out. When he got to room 227, he noticed the rooms luxury right away. There was an entertainment center complete with a T.V., DVD player and stereo. There was one queen size bed in the living room and one in a bedroom. It also had a small refrigerator that he could put some beer in. He thought to his self – this nigga is going to fill this mutha fucka up with beer and he's buying the first round of drinks, I ain't paying for this shit by myself. He turned the T.V on BET, he was like yeah I can fuck with this. 106 and Park had just started and he was ready to get the party started. So he laid out one of the fits he and Tia had chosen and began to get ready for a shower.

Then he thought, this nigga Jason might show up while I'm in the shower so he called the clerk at the front desk and told her that Jason would be the second occupant and to give him a key. It was 10 minutes to 4:00. By the time he got out the shower, sure enough Jason had made it. He was putting his bags away so the room didn't look too crowded. Jason said "ay this is pretty fuckin nice, this'll be way better than those barracks". Tim said "Hell yeah, that's the first time I didn't have a muther fucker timing my shower. Man where the hell you been?" Jason said. "Shit, I had to get a couple things for the wife. You know to make sure the home coming will be extra special – you know what I'm talking about Playboy! And I went to Budget and got us a rental. Tim said, "Hell yah man, that's why you made Sergeant. You're always ready for some shit." Yeah man, that way if were too hung over in the morning, we can sleep in and still make it to the airport. Yea, well you gone be proud of your boy. I pulled this little fine ass broad. She said she wants to show me how to have a good time in LA. I was goin to ask her about some friends but I know your ass would've got spooked. Jason said, "Nah man I'm good, you better hope she ain't one of them set up hoes". He said, "Nah man I peeped her. She's kinda classy. She wants me to call her when we're ready to go." "Hey that whats up. But right now I'm about to hit this water and get pressed. You know what I'm talking about," Jason said laying out one of his outfits. "Fo sure! Anyway my nigga you get anything to eat yet, I'm about to order up some food. No I didn't. Why don't you order a grip of shit-cause I'm starving and I plan on doing a whole lot of drinking. For sure – Fore sure.

# TIA

Tim waited until it got a little later before giving Tia a call. He didn't want to seem like she was his only option. So when he called her, he had the music playing loud in the background. When she answered he said, 'Hey what's happening with you Pretty lady?" She said, "What's good?" Not to much, I was just about to head out and I wanted to see if you had come up with any plans for a lonely man out here in a foreign land. She said, "Oh this is Tim, I was beginning to think you weren't going to have anytime for me. Ah-Nah, for sure I was going to check in with you. Like I said, I have an ideal of how to get around, but I'm sure I'll have a better time with an escort. She said, "so you think I'm an escort"? "No not like that," he said, "damm ma I'm going to have to be careful choosing my words with you. She said, "baby I'm just playing with you. I've already been there – done that and believe me if I was still in the game – I wouldn't be working in no department store." Tim said, yeah that sounds interesting, maybe you can tell me about some of your business dealings and adventures later on." She said, "yeah maybe. Where are you staying, I'm going to come get you?" he said, "hold on Pretty Girl, I told you I'm with my partna. Why don't you just give me some directions and I'll meet you there. We'll grab a couple of Shirley temples and you can tell me a little bit about yourself." Tia said, "Cool, I didn't know you were mobile. Okay then, the place is called the Century club and it is on Century Boulevard near LAX. Make sure you save my number just in case you need more directions. Tim said, "I'm with that. I'll see you there.

As Jason pulled the Jeep commander into the parking lot, he noticed that he didn't have too much of a hard time finding a spot. He said, "man it looks like this is it. But it doesn't look like it's too live to me." Tim said. "Yeah man it's only 9:30, I'm gonna see if Baby is bull shitting. If shit ain't poppin in a little bit we can go." While they were standing in front of the club waiting in line, Tim naturally checked his surroundings to asses the situation for the possibility of a problem occurring. Although they were in the heart of LA, people weren't dressed like gang bangers as he expected. Everyone was pretty much in business casual attire. Some even in three piece suits and high fashion evening gowns. He himself had chosen to wear a white polo style Sean John shirt, with black Sean John Jeans, some white expensive 310's tennis shoes that Tia had convinced him to buy. Jason was wearing a black Italio Mundo dress shirt, with matching gray slacks. He set if off with a pair of black square toed Georgio Brutinis." he asked Tim, Do you think everything is straight? Tim said, "I think we are straight. I'd feel better if I had Back Back with me. 'Back back was Tim's 40 caliber Smith and Wesson. "But if we have some funk, our odds look pretty good."

After they were searched and paid the door they noticed that the club had had only one way in and one way out. Besides that the place was kind of up scale. It had a live DJ and two bars. It also had a stage suggesting they hosted live bands some nights. There was a large dance floor, several tables and a few booths. They even had 4 pool tables in the back. Jason yelled, "Shit it looks like your girl has a little taste." Tim leaned over and said, "Yeah my dude. This don't look to bad at all. Let's go get a spot at the bar. When they finally got the bar tenders attention. Tim ordered 2 shots of Tanquray and 2 bottles of MGD. Tim raised his shot and proposed a toast. Here's to all of the good times ahead. Jason agreed, he said, "Yes may we never see a desert again unless it's in the Nevada Valley." With that they bottomed out.

Tim followed his shot with a big gulp of beer. He immediately ordered 2 more shots of Tanguray. Jason just casually sipped his beer and realized once again he would be designated the responsible party. Tim let out a loud shout- wooh! He said, "Damm Lay Low you know if it wasn't for you, I wouldn't have made it back to this mutha fucka alive." Jason knew Tim must already be feeling the alcohol. Lay Low was a name Tim would call Jason when telling the story of an incident that had happened in Rahmadi in which Tim would give him more credit than was deserved him, because he was just doing his job. But this time he didn't mind, it was a celebration. Jason said, "yah man you really made that name stick. Tim said, "that's you my nigga! I didn't even know you and that God dammed Tali Whacker was about to take me out. All I know is I heard that 50 cal start bucking, I looked up, like what the fuck and you was like lay low-lay low!

Jason laughed a little bit, he was feeling a little elated. He said, "this dude is crazy." Tim Feeling a little more excited continued to give him more praise. He was like, "for real cousin-what was it like 4 or 5 of those mutha-fuckers. I didn't even see them and they were going to take me out. But you was like clack-clack-clack-clack-clack-clack! Tim didn't notice but he was getting kind of hype. He had accidentally bumped into a guy that was trying to holler at this girl sitting next to him at the bar. The dude was like 'Damn Blood, you better calm that shit down a couple of notches. Do you see me standing here nigga?" Not being one to back down from a challenge, Tim quickly turned around and said calmly, "what's your problem nigga?" The dude said, "nigga you got one more time to bump into me and you going to be the one who has a problem!" Tim went to snap back like, "check this out – but Jason snatched him back and stood in between them.

Jason said, "ay my man, he didn't mean no disrespect. We're having a little celebration, we just got back from Iraq and he's a little excited. The dude said, "well blood better calm the fuck down. Just cause y'all made it through Iraq don't mean you gone make it through this park called Loudus." Jason ignored him and said, "yeah, your right-but like I said he didn't mean no harm." The dude shrugged his shoulders and turned back around.

Tim was highly pissed. He said, damm man, you didn't even have to do that shit. You should've let me smash that lil mutha fucker." Jason said, "Nah man, that's not what we're here for. You need to keep your eyes on the prize, you have better things to do than to roll around on the floor with that nigga." Tim said, "I wasn't going to roll around with him. I was going to break that Nigga's jaw and that was...." Umh umh.

Tim was rudely interrupted again. This time, it was by a pretty browned skinned girl. Her hair was pressed and pulled to one side. She had a short sleeved white collared button up the middle shirt, that barely contained her breast. She had on a short black tennis skirt and some four inch stilettos. She said, "I see you don't waste no time trying to meet people". He said, "Tia?" with a puzzled face because he wasn't sure if it was her. She said, "Yeah-it's me" she had gotten the response she had hoped fore. He said, "Damm, you look good baby. I don't know that nigga," he said But if that nigga comes at me sideways again, he's going to get to know me." She said, "don't pay that shit no attention, can't nothing good come from that situation. Besides that, isn't this supposed to be a celebration?" He said, "yeah-yeah-yeah-yeah. This is my partna Sergeant Lay Low. You can thank him for my black ass being here, he saved my ass on many occasions. She stuck her hand out and said, "I'm Tia. Please to meet you." "I'm Jason, he said, "the pleasure is mine".

He said, "Yeah my boy seems to think you're the next best thing going, short of Christ's returning to earth." She said, "is that right?: Looking at Tim. "You need some healing baby?" Tim said, "I might have mentioned a couple of things about you, nothing to major though. He looked her up and down, swallowed his shot of Tanguray and said, "let me buy you a drink." Tia said, "I'll have a 7up. I don't drink alcohol." Now this took Tim by surprise, because his plan was to get bent then go back to the room and show Tia how he had learned to demo walls. He said "oh you're one of those Good Girls." She said, "I'm good at what I do," and stared him down right in the eyes. Tim said, "Umh" realizing he was not going to win that stare contest. He said, "What about you Lay Low, you want something to drink?" Jason said, "I'm good for now." Tim ignored him and told the bar tender to get Tia's drink, 2 more shots and 2 more beers. She quickly brought them back and he gave her a five dollar tip. The music in the background was bumping, *Shortie won't a Thug_ bottles in tha club. Shortie wanna hump*

# THE CHASE

Tia took the shot glass out of Tim's hand, grabbed him with her other hand and said, "come dance with me." He followed her to the dance floor, she turned around and began to back that thang up on him. She reached up to hold him by the back of his head. With her free hand then grabbed his hand and placed it on her stomach. Tim was quickly aroused from the soft brushes of her ass on his groin. He grabbed her by the waist and pulled her closer, then spoke in her ear. He said, "so what's good with you Ma, is this your get away spot?" She said, "I like to come here because they usually have a older crowd. They only have one Hip hop night and not to many people know about it." He said, "so how does a man let a woman as fine as you, get away from him and to the club dressed like this without him? Or do you have a man?" she shook her head no, she said, "I'm not really in to men right now. I have a girlfriend. I've been with her for almost a year, but right now that bitch is trippen." She turned to face him put her arms around his neck and said, "is that going to be a problem for you?"

*Shortie wanna hump. You know I like to touch, your lovely lady lumps.* He took a gulp, grabbed her by the waist, let one hand slide down to palm her ass. He said, "no that's not a problem at all." She said, "So what else were you planning on getting into tonight?" He said, "let me word this carefully. My every intention was to get into you tonight." She could feel his love muscle press against her stomach. She looked him square in the eyes with a sexy smile and said "that's what's up." After a couple of songs, Tim lead her off of the dance floor back to the bar and lay Low was still sipping. Tim asked him is everything alright? Jason said, "yeah I'm good, but that dude man, them niggas is like eight deep now. Them mutha fuckas keep mean muggin and shit." Tia said, "Yeah them are some hatin ass niggas. I'm ready to get up outta here anyway." Jason said, "Yeah I'm with that, we can shake if ya'll want to.

When they got out to the car there was a larger group of individuals hanging in the parking lot. They were sitting on the hoods of the cars and hollering at the girls headed into the club. Tia said "yeah it's time to go. Now them Crip niggas is getting deep, It's about to be some shit." Jason said, "so you wanna call it a night my man?" Tim thought for a minute and then said. "Nah I wanted to check out that Santa Monica Pier that we passed earlier. Do you remember how to get there?" He said "vaguely". Tim said, "well I'm gonna ride with Baby, Just follow us." Jason said "Cool." Tim said "baby let me drive." As they were approaching the highway to head back toward Santa Monica, Tim was coming up on a yellow light. He smashed the gas to the floor of Tia's Nissan Maxima and went through it. Tia said "He ain't going to be able to make that light." Tim continued to look forward, smiled and said, "he wasn't suppose to."

As they stepped into the motel room, Tim could barely contain his excitement. Tia had been groping his pants the whole way there. He grabbed her by the small of her back then kissed her and pressed her body against his. He then slipped his hand under her skirt and felt her round bare ass. He let out a moan of excitement and thought damm she may be more ready for this than me. He then picked her up with her holding on to the back of his neck and to kiss him. He carried her to the bedroom and layed her on her back. He began to unbutton each button down the front of her shirt releasing her firm round flawless breast. When he saw her dark pointed nipples, he grabbed them firmly and gave her one last kiss on the mouth before moving to her breast. He than began to make circles around her left nipple with his tongue. As Tia let out a moan he moved to the right nipple and continued to circle the left with his finger.

Tia said "Oh baby, damm that feels good!" she was rubbing his back. Tim then pulled her to the edge of the bed and lifted her skirt over her stomach. He now knew he was wrong about her being without underwear because he had revealed a white laced cotton thong. He was careful pulling it down and over her high heeled stilettos. He quickly returned to give her a passionate kiss in her most intimate of spots. He began to glide his tongue back and fourth across her clitoris. He could feel her response, because she began to drown his tongue in her juices and she ground her hips against his tongue. She rubbed her breast and said "Oh I'm coming, don't stop." Tim thought to his self, damm I know. She then sat up, snatching off her shirt and said, "I want you inside of me." Tim quickly obliged. He stood up, took off his shirt and kicked off his shoes. He then pulled his remaining clothes to the floor. Tia crawled back on to the bed. Tim grabbed his dick in his hand and said, "This shit here ain't nothing to play with. She raised her knees in the air, began rubbing her pussy and said "Daddy, I can take it." Tim got on top of her and placed the head of his dick inside her. He began to pump but he found her to be tighter than what he was use to. He then kind of forcefully jammed more into her and she let out a painful moan. He kissed her on the mouth and said "it's okay ma" then preceded to reintroduce her to the joys of being with a man.

# LAY LOW

After finding his way back into Santa Monica, Jason got to the Pier and searched the parking lot for Tia's Maxima. After searching for a while with no luck, he decided that he had been abandoned just like he had suspected. Tim thought shit like that was funny. He thought, Man all he had to do was tell me what was up and I would have given him some space.

Walking along the beach for awhile, his resentment was turning to anger. He was more intoxicated then he had realized. It had been a long day and all he wanted to do was get to sleep so that he'd be ready to go in the morning. He decided to go back to the room because tomorrow couldn't come quick enough for him. When he walked in the room, he noticed it was just as they had left it. He didn't realize that they were already there until he heard Tia's moans coming from the room. He laughed to himself and thought, this mutha fucka is a fool. He took off his shirt and shoes, laid in the bed and tried to ignore the escapade that was going on in the next room. Then all of a sudden there was silence. He closed his eye and tried to concentrate on sleep, he was immediately interrupted by a series of slapping sounds and Tia moaning louder than ever. He jumped up with steam coming from his ears. He slammed the door to the bedroom and turned the stereo on to help drown out the pounding Tim must have been givin Tia. It was coming up on 2:00am.

Just about 7am, Jason sprung up from an almost drunkin induced coma. It had been a while since he could drink carelessly like that and last night would hold a high place in his record book. Instinctively, his game plan began to come back to him He was to iron his Nautica slacks and shirt, take a quick shower and get dressed. He was out of there by 9 o'clock. He wasn't going to put up with any of Tim's games. Come rain, sleet, or snow he was going to be with his wife today. As Jason was ironing his clothes, the door to the room opened up. When he looked up, Tia was came out wearing nothing but her birthday suit. He looked back down at his pants acting as if he hadn't seen her. "I see you found your way back okay", she said. Trying to play cool, Jason said, "I figured ya'll would want to be alone. Not wanting her to know that he was to upset, he continued, "I knew that nigga was up to something." He was getting a full view o Tia's flawless hour glass figure. He tightened his jaw – said damm to himself and focused back on the task at hand. Tia said, "yeah we were just having some fun with you." She continued on her way to the restroom. Lay Low heard the toilet flush then looked up to see Tia emerge wearing the biggest smile. She yawned and stretched, shifted her hips and said, "Yeah, we were just playing." Lay Low said, "Tell that dude that I said he has about an hour before I ride out of here with or without him. She cut her eyes at him, curled her lips and said, "Um huh." Then walked into the room.

Lay Low shook his head in amazement. He said out loud, "I've got to hurry up and get my ass home." After he finished ironing, he went and got into the shower. When he came out he saw Tim sitting in the chair rubbing his stomach, wearing only his boxers. Jason said, "so now you've decided to stay here." Tim said "Hell nah man, she's gone." Jason said, "Yeah well you think your ass is funny, we'll see how funny it is when I'm on that plane and your still here trying to be a porn star." He said, "nigga you ain't leaving me here! I already pressed my shit yesterday, all I have to do is hit that water. Jason said, "Well you better hit that shit, cause come 9 o'clock I'm outta here." Tim said, "Nigga don't be hatin on me. I told you she had some home girls, you're the one scared your wife is gone find out or something." Jason said, "man I ain't worried about her finding out. It's about me knowing. Me and my wife have a bond and when we're together there is an unexplainable feeling we have. I would never compromise that trust and respect for a physical act with some hooker I just met. Tim said, "I feel you." Jason said, "you do?" Tim said, "Yeah I feel you. But it was just something about her ass man, it just kept calling me." They both laughed. Jason said, "I'm going to load the truck. You need to get ready so we can raise up outta here." Tim said, "Fo sure."

On their way to the airport, Lay Low asked. "So when you get home are you going to try to patch things up with that chick Anita? Or what are you going to do?" Tim said, "Na man I'm cool on that broad, if something would have happen to me over there she wouldn't have even known. I tried to many times to contact her and she didn't even respond." Lay Low said, "Well what was she supposed to do after she found out you was messing with her sister?" Tim snapped back, "Man, she was messing with me!" Lay Low said "Man, you got a lot of growing up to do." Tim ignored him and continued, "I'm going to see how my brother is getting along. Then I'm going to school, I'm going to open my own business doing property maintenance. What about you?" Jason said, "After I consummate my marriage vowels, and perform my God given duty to my wife for about a week or two, my uncle has a job set up for me working for GM."

They had pulled up to the Budget that was located at the Airport and were beginning to put their bags onto the dollies provided. Then they quickly checked in their baggage, and headed to the terminal from which their flight would depart. Jason said, "After you get settled, are you going to contact Tia?" Tim said, "I don't know man. Tia was cool for a good time, but I wouldn't try to build anything with her. There are plenty of Tia's in the town. Jason said, "One of these days you are going to realize that you have lost a lot of good women." The intercom bursted in "Flight 4109, destination Denver, Colorado at Denver International Airport now boarding."

When they got off the plane in Denver Jason and Tim went to retrieve Tim's baggage. Standing by the baggage claim was Tim's younger brother

Clarence. Clarence was wearing a big smile, black jeans, a white Tee and a black baseball cap to the back. As Tim got closer, Clarence stood at attention and gave him a salute. Tim was very happy to see his brother, he said, "cut the games man." And jabbed for his stomach. Clarence laughed and pulled his brother in for a heartfelt hug. He said, "Man it's good to see you Playboy." Tim said, Yeah I'm glad to see you're here. I was going to be pissed off if I had to pay for a cab." Clarence said, "Man I told you I'd be here. Your the only family I've got, there ain't no way I was going to let you down." Tim said, "Ay Bro, this is my partner Lay Low I told you about. He said, "Lay Low this is Clarence." Jason stuck his hand out, he said, "I'm glad to finally meet you. I've heard alot of shit about you." Clarence replied, "Well if it had something to do with getting some money or some Flat Back fucking, it was probably true. Jason said, "Wow- Tim's got a mini Me." They all laughed. Clarence asked Lay Low, "So what's up, are you going to hit the town with us for awhile?" Jason said, "Nah my Man, I've got my family expecting me in a few hours. My layover is only for a hour." Clarence said, "Well it might be a little longer than that. Since that shit happened in Seattle, they raised the Terror Alert and all the flights have been getting backed up." Tim said, "What happened in Seattle?" Clarence said, "Ya'll didn't hear about that shit?" He said, "some crazy mutha fuckas blew up a Microsoft manufacturing plant, killed like 43 people." Tim said, "Hell nah. When did this happen?" Clarence said, "I guess sometime this morning. You know I haven't seen the news, but these airport securities have been sweating the shit out of me." Jason said, "do they know who did it?" Clarence said, "I don't know man, all I have is second hand information. Look your plane doesn't start loading for an hour. Why don't ya'll let me buy ya'll a welcome home drink and we can see what's on the news?"

As they were approaching the food court, they noticed the heightened since of attention coming from the Security staff. There were extra check points and uniformed officers with dogs patrolling. They walked into a nice restaurant that had a bar in the waiting area and a couple of TV's turned to CNN. They took seats closes to the T.V. to try to hear what was going on. The news anchor said, "Once again, we do have 43 people confirmed dead. There are still up to 25 unaccounted for – so that number could rise. This is a Microsoft warehouse in the southern portion of the city. The FBI, ATF and dozens of emergency personnel are on the scene. We will give you more information as it becomes available.

Tim said, "well ain't that some shit. It's like this shit don't never stop. The bartender, a pretty-petite blond head girl said, "Can I get you gentleman anything to drink?" Clarence said, "Yeah, we'll have 3 beers, whatever you have on tap will be fine." As she was drawing the beers she said, "Those poor people. You'd think they'd be ready to prevent something like this after the 9/11 attacks. I feel sorry for their families." Jason said, "Yeah it really is a shame. Tim said, "One day they'll get it right." She said, "Let me know if you need anything else. Clarence said, "so what's on the agenda Bro? I have all of the homeboy's on stand by. They want to know where the party is going to be." Tim said, "What homeboy's are you talking about?" Clarence said, "what do you mean? The Clique nigga. You know the homies ain't went no where."

Tim hadn't heard much from or about the 'Cash Clique' since he had went into basic training. They were a gang of bandits Tim and Clarence had helped organize to keep other hustlers out of Aurora. They felt that since they had been raised there and had practically created the drug market. There was no way they were going to let outsiders come and reap the benefits. Tim had been a pretty ruthless dude coming up in the A-Town. All he had was his brother and Mother to care for. Once he was involved in the Drug game, he was able to provide a pretty good living for his family. Tim's world had came crashing down on him when his Mom suddenly died from heart failure. They didn't even know she had had complications. He always wanted to prove to his Mom that she had raised a good man. He would always tell her, "Mom watch I'm going to leave this hustling alone. I'm going to join the Service and do something with my life." She never would get a chance to see him fulfill his promise. When Tim attended his mother's funeral, it was the first time in a long time that he had been in a church. He was overcome with emotion and he felt God had spoken to him directly. It was at that moment that he made another promise to God and his Mother to make good on all the promises he had made before.

Clarence said, "Yeah Mr. AZ, we've been waiting for you to touch down, we have a lot of shit going on." Jason said, "Who the fuck is Mr. AZ?" Tim said, "Man I have forgotten all about that shit. Before I went to boot camp I had been following the war. They said this dude Abu Mussah Al Zarowaquai was the leader of Al Qaeda in Iraq. He was giving our boys hell over there. I took that name because we were giving these suckas and the Aurora police hell over here." Jason said, "WOW." Clarence said, "Nigga you mean to tell me you haven't been representing." Tim started laughing and said, "Nigga them mutha fuckas don't give a fuck about no mutha fuckin Cash Clique! The only thing I was representing was my ass, so I could save it. He took a big drink of his beer. Lay Low said, "yeah that shit ain't no joke over there." Tim said, "Anyways Playboy. After you get everything situated at home, make sure you let me know. I'm still going to fly out there so we can get together on some of what we talked about." Lay Low said, "No doubt."

Passenger flight 4179 will start boarding in 15 minutes. "That sound's like my 'cue' said Jason. "to bad I didn't get a chance to kick it with you Clarence." Clarence said, "Man you've got big things poppin, and little shit cracking." He said, "their will be plenty of time for that. You know home comes first." As they were making their way back to the terminal Tim admitted. "I'm not too good at Good-byes. So just remember this, your like a big brother to me. So if you ever need anything Playboy, you give a nigga a call." Jason returned. "That's really heart felt homeboy, the same goes to you. And I wish you success in your business endeavors and everything you do." They hugged each other and said "One", then went their separate ways.

After picking up Tim's luggage from the baggage claim, Clarence was leading the way. He stopped in the parking lot in back of a burgundy Navigator and started to load Tim's bags. Tim was like, "Oh shit nigga-who's shit are you pushing? Clarence said, "What do you mean? This is my shit, Man your little Bro has been putting it down since you've been gone." Tim said, "damm-are those some 28"'s?" Clarence said, "You like those Mr. AZ?" "Yeah their alright but watch when you see the footwear on my Camaro. Tim said, "you have a Camaro too?" Clarence said, "Yeah man – I have a Navy Blue Camaro with the Chrome flakes sittin on some 20" Lexani's. Nigga when I turn the knob on that piece, mutha fuckas be reporting small tremblers throughout the whole city. Mr. AZ said, "Bullshit nigga. How did you come up on some shit like that?" Clarence said, "I don't have no bullshit for you my nig."

As they were getting into the truck Clarence said, "That's what I need to tell you about. Do you remember that Mexican broad Jackie I used to fuck with back in high school?" Tim asked, "Are you talking about when you went to Hinkley?" Clarence said, "Yeah" Tim said, "I never met her, but yeah I remember who your talking about." Clarence said, Anyway I had ran back into her at the Mall with her home girls. So I hook up with the bitch and we're kickin it pretty tough. One day we're over one of her Aunt's, celebrating her cousin's quince era and she was introducing me to some of her people." "Man some of her cousin's that had came down from Greely started this poker game. So I get in nigga, and I started knocking 'em off. So it had came down to me and her oldest cousin Pedro." I was up like $700 and dude didn't have no more cash on him. So I forced his call and dude was like let me put in my watch to cover the bet. He was betting on a Royal Flush, I had 5 jacks my nig. Broke him. To make a long story short, the nigga didn't wanna come off the watch, so he takes me out to his car and says why don't we make a deal! Man the nigga comes out of the center console with a half ounce of powder. I'm talking about some P. Funk my nig. So I'm weighting the watch against the work, and I'm like hell yeah – that's a way better flip. Mr. AZ interrupted and said, "Man that's the same shit you were doing when I left. You can't tell me you're living like this off of pushing no work." Clarence said, "Hell nah man it ain't nothing like when you left. Man come to find out – this nigga Pedro has more bricks than the county jail." Tim said, "Are you serious?" Clarence said, "I bullshit you not my nig. And that shit was on time. You know after Mom died, I was going through some shit. Then you just up and left. Man I didn't know what I was going to do." Tim said, "You know I didn't mean to leave you on your own Lil bro, that was just something I had to do." "I understand what you did," Clarence said. "But you know I had some decisions to make too. You know I can't get a real job with that felony I caught for that strap. So I decided I was gone ball – until I fall, cause I damn sure ain't gonna crawl. You understand me?" Tim said, "Damn Clarence you're lucky. Shit like that always falls into your lap." Clarence said, "Not really nigga. What's up with this Clarence shit? Your back at home now call me C-Loc nigga." Tim just shook his head and laughed.

C-Loc said, "I got some cush already twisted up for you in the ash tray. Go on and spark that shit up." Tim said, "Nigga I don't smoke that shit no more." C-Loc said, "What! Fuck it – that's cool. I know I'm about to smoke it." He said, "What you know about this-"as he turned up his stereo. He was playing Above the Law. 'Black Superman' *has anybody seen him – Black super man, yeah, yeah...*

As they were pulling into MR. AZ condominium complex, his home sickness kicked in and he remembered how long it had been since he left his home. His two bedroom, two level luxury condo was located on the Southside of Aurora. His Chevy Tahoe was stored in his private garage which was adjacent to his unit. C-Loc broke him out of his thoughts. He said, "Welcome home my nigga. It's alright man, you made it." Tim said, "Yeah. Man it wasn't easy. And there ain't nothing like returning to a house where the Home Owner Association keeps my grass cut and the maintenance of my property up. You know what I'm sain Playboy?" C-Loc said, "Yeah man. You made a good investment in this mutha-fucka. You deserve the best man, you always have made good decisions."

As Tim took out his keys, he said jokingly, "Let's see if these still work." When he entered the living room, it was like a blast from the past. Everything looked as it did the day he left to report for is deployment. C-Loc came in behind him carrying some of his bags. He commented "you got over like a Fat Cat paying only 110 for this." Tim had the living room decked out with a Tan leather sectional. He had a black lacquer Coffee Table and matching end tables. His 42" flat screen T.V. sat on a black storage case which held his CD and DVD collection. The extra bedroom was converted into a home gym. His master bedroom was located upstairs with his private restroom. Their was also a loft that overlooked the living room that he used as an office space.

Tim said, "I finally get to stretch out and relax in my own shit!" C-Loc said, "Don't get to relaxed, we still have to get you screwed, blewed, and tattooed before morning. Nigga we're about to have some fun." Mr. AZ said, "I might just chill at the house today, take some time to get my head right." C-Loc said, "You don't feel like leaving? Don't trip." He pulled out his Nextel, then hit his chirper. He said, "Wes West my nigga"? Their partner Teflon chirped in and said, "Wes Wit it"? They felt like every time they left the house they were watched and immulated by everyone in the town. So they always put on a show. He chirped in "Are ya'll on ya'lls way?" C-Loc chirped back – Nah man, there's been a change in plans. Have Tonya and Dana pack everything up and ya'll meet us at Mr. AZ's. Teflon said, "Damn what's the problem?" He said, "Ain't no problem, we're just going to get down over here." Teflon said, "Aright. Call the rest of them Nigga's and tell them you changed the plans. I'll be there in 15 minutes. Tim said, "Tell what niggas? Man what the hell you got going on?" C-Loc said, "Man you know the homies are waiting to see you. We just planned a little get together to welcome you home. Man the homies been missing you or did you forget you had friends?" Tim said, "Nah Man, it's all good." C-Loc said, "Oh yeah I almost forgot. He went out to the truck and returned with the rest of Tim's luggage. He tossed Tim a small box containing a Nextel phone. He said, "I went ahead and got you a Gossiper hooked up and you know its some more shit on the way."

Tim said, "Ay that was thoughtful of you lil Bro. But I have to tell you, I'm not the same person that left here 20 months ago. I put me an agenda together and I'm not going to have time for none of that shit I was into before I left." C-Loc said, "That's cool man. You don't have to do anything you don't want to. You know I have your back on whatever you get into." Tim said, "Yeah that's what's up. I have this money for school; I'm going to take this Business Management course so I can open my property maintenance business as soon as possible." C-Loc being quick to jump on the band wagon like he always did with his big brother said, "That would be tight." You know I've been coaching these little league teams, I'm not just a hustler I don't want to be doing this shit forever neither. Tim said, "You don't need to. I don't want to see your ass in jail or worse." C-Loc said, "Real talk – I've been looking for something to invest in to – to make some legal paper. I just have a few more..... C-Loc was interrupted by the sound of Teflon revving up his motorcycle. Teflon got off of his bike and removed his helmet. Tim came out of the house to greet him. Teflon gave him a hard five and said, "What's up Mr. AZ, good to see you home!" Mr. AZ said, "Yeah my man, it's good to be home." Teflon said, "Why didn't you wanna come check out our spot?" He said, "It's not that, I just have some shit to take care of here. I didn't know ya'll had this shit planned." Teflon said, "Man you're my nigga, you know I fucks with you hard. And I got some bitches thats been waiting to meet you." Mr. AZ said, "That's cool man, as long as this shit don't get out of hand. You know I have to live here."

C-Loc was coming from his Navigator carrying a book of CD's. He said, "Nigga don't trip. You know we don't fuck with nobody but the Clique. It's going to be a few bitches to cook and what not, but that's it. Come check out this new CD some young niggas made coming out of the Town." C-Loc put on the CD and turned the stereo up until it could be heard outside. He lit up the blunt that he was smoking on earlier. He said to Teflon, "This nigga don't smoke no more." Teflon said, "Why not you have to take UA's or something?" Mr. AZ said, "Nah, I'm just cool on that shit." Teflon took out a large sack of some Purple Cush, and said, "Well I hope you don't mind cause I'm about to smoke all of this shit." Tonya and Dana were pulling in and Dana decided to reverse in so her Suburban would be easier to unload. Dana said to Teflon, "I packed everything, can you come help us unload it?" He said, "Damn just take the shit in there. It's not like that shit is heavy. Get everything set up and I'll start the fire for you." Tonya was carrying in some covered pots and pans. She said, "Teflon I don't know who you think you are, you can at least grab those coolers." Teflon said, "Both of ya'll just grab one side, the shit ain't that hard." He turned back to Mr. AZ he said, "she has some ass under that dress, your brother be sleeping on her. All you gotta do is get in her ear I bet you can fuck." Mr. AZ said, "That's good to know, but I'm not trippen on that shit right now. I have some business to take care of before I get wrapped up with any of these broads." Teflon said, "Oh, you want some of that 'Nita' huh? You been thinking about fucking with her again? Shit ya'll were like Siamese twins – couldn't catch you two niggas apart."

Mr. AZ got into his feelings but he held his composure. He said, "I'm not thinking about that trick. As far as she knows – I could be dead and buried out there in that desert." I'm glad to hear you say that cousin. I didn't want to be the one to tell you, but she's fucking with this old square ass nigga. I guess it's pretty serious too, that nigga lives with her and everything. Mr. AZ said, "Well I'm not trippen. You win some and you lose some. But I promise you I've won more than I lost. Shit let's go see how much ass ol girl is hiding under that dress."

26

# ANITA

By the time C-Loc was getting the ribs on the grill, Active and Static had showed up with three more shorties. The shorties were quick to make their selves comfortable; two of them made drinks and pulled up to the domino game. The other was breaking down some weed. Active had given her to roll. Tim had been bothered by what Teflon had told him about Anita. He couldn't believe that she had completely gotten over him and had moved on. Even though he was getting a lot of attention from the women his partners had brought over, his mind was focused on Anita. So he came up with a plan to see if what he'd heard was true. He said to Teflon, "What kind of Bike is that that you pulled up on?" Teflon said "it's just a Kawasaki Ninja. It's a 1500 though; I can hold my own on that mutha fucka." Tim said "yeah it looks pretty nice. Why don't you let your boy hit a couple of corners on it. You know to see if I still got it." Teflon said "Oh that ain't no problem cousin. But you know all it is is riding a bike, once you learn you never forget." He said this as he was pulling out the keys and tossing them to the person who he respected like a big brother. Tim told him, "Shit I just want to work out some cob webs, see what's going on in the city." Teflon said "You know I ain't trippin cousin. You know what's mine is yours. It was just as Teflon said, everything came back to him. After he keyed the ignition and hit the starter button the bike came to life beneath him. He revved the gas a little to get a feel for it before coasting backwards away from the parking position. After his helmet was secure, he did a minor peal out of the parking lot and into the early evening traffic. Once he was

27

free on the open road there was no stopping him. He was acting a fool as he darted in and out of traffic in a hurry to get no where.

In the rush hour traffic he even passed the cars stopped at red lights by riding in between them on the yellow margin lines. This was a huge turn around from the heavy duty Humvies he had been driving lately. But now it was time to see why a woman whom he'd given so much of his self to was able to walk away from him so easily. Sure he had made a huge mistake by finally giving in to her sisters persistent attempts to seduce him. But they had made it through much worse things. Like when he had convinced her and her friend to set up these out of town hustlers. And after the robbery they had to bring back the 10G's because the niggas didn't fall for her home girls story and had taken her hostage. Tim had to risk his life bringing the money back because Anita's friend had forgotten to mention she took one of the niggas to her home to fuck him. Tim really had needed that money and didn't care about this dizzy broad who had been careless in setting up the jack. As long as it wasn't Nita he was cool. But Nita flashed on him for about 3 hours before he decided to give them their money back. He felt like she cared more about her friends life then his. It would be a long two months before they would work that out. By now he was pulling out of rush hour traffic onto the side streets. After a few turn's he would be in front of her house located in a secluded northern Aurora neighborhood.

As he pulled up to the stop sign on her corner he could see Nita making her way to a brand new Cadillac STS. He could see the features that came together to form her beautiful face from the corner. Her house was the third one down. But he could also see a huge change in her. Almost instantly, some light skinned buster with some fake ass dread locks wearing glasses emerged from the house. After carefully shutting the door he rushed to Anita's side. Taking her by the small of her back and her right hand he led her to and opened the car door. By the size of her bulging belly she probably needed the help. Tim felt as if he were being stabbed in the heart with an ice pick. Any hope of getting his girl back leaked from his soul with every stab. Once again he revved up the muscle of the machine beneath him before he rode past his one and only true love. He felt as if she knew it was him as she watched him drive by, but still he didn't say a word..... He decided that it would be best for him to just head home.

The sun was getting ready to set, but they had no intentions on slowing down. The music still blaring in the back ground – E-40 and Too Short, *We started, with nothing, from nothing we make something. Nobody really gave a damn about us. From the ground on up!* C-Loc came in and turned down the music and said "Ay bro-this is something else we have to do. This is just a little somethan – somethan now that your back in the Town to let these suckas know where your from. He came from behind his back with a gold Figaro chain, with two capital letter C's hanging from it. It had 2 quarter-karat diamonds to punctuate the C's. Mr. AZ put on a smile and said "That's how you're going to do it? Just have me put my shit on blast." C-Loc said "nah my nig – you ain't on blast. Niggas know you're a factor when they see that. He reached through the collar of his white "T" and pulled out an identical chain. He said "I got mine. Static and Active both revealed identical chains and Static said "you know I keeps my shit on deck." Teflon pulled out his and said "I got mine." Then he raised up his shirt to show his P-89 ruger then continued, "And I have something for a nigga who has a problem with it." Mr. AZ nodded his head and said, "Aight." Dana said, "come on Teflon, it's your play."

# WELCOME HOME JASON

After unboarding the plane in Detroit, Jason was ecstatic to see his beautiful wife. Even though he had pictures of her and had visited her through a live web feed, nothing could compare with sharing the same space and air with her. She was 5 foot 4 from the floor, with breast that stood at attention better than half of his platoon. She had her hair pulled back into a bun, which brought out the thickness of her eyebrows and eyelashes. Her hazel brown eyes seemed almost unreal against the back drop of her dark brown skin. She had made a careful selection in picking out her pine green form fitting dress and a pair of sandals that laced half way up to her knees.

While waiting, she stood holding a small hand made sign that said, "Welcome Home Sgt. Hephner". Next to her was Jason's lovely mom who had tears of joy coming from her eyes. Jason's uncle Richard had also showed up for the home coming. He looked kind of silly standing a 6 foot 4 inches holding a bundle of balloons. Every since Jason's father had fallen out of the picture, and he had left seven year old Jason and his mom to fend for themselves. Uncle Richard had stepped in to be the positive male figure in Jason's life. Richard had been the one to get Jason to football practice, the one who had gotten him interested in track and field in high school. He also had taught Jason how to use his awkward height and weight to an advantage in school yard fights. He had never had any children of his own. So to see his one and only nephew returning home from a deadly war as a Sergeant in the United States Marines made him feel as proud as any father. Seeing the fruits of his labor made him smile like he never had before.

As Jason approached his wife, a couple of her own tears had began to weld in her eyes. He dropped his bags to the floor and she leaped into his arms. She rested her head on his chest as her tears began to flow relentlessly. She said, "Sugar I'm so glad you're finally home." He held her tight, almost off of her feet. He said, "I missed you too Angel." She gave him a little kiss on the mouth, but managed to sneak in that little trick with her tongue that Jason had craved so many nights while he was away from home. Just as he had released her, his mom stepped in and said, "Baby, I'm glad your home. I don't know what I would've did if something happened to you." Jason let her go, then wiped a tear from her face. He said, "Momma you know I wasn't going to let nothing happen to me." Richard then pulled his nephew in for and embrace. He said, "You know you have made your family very proud son." Jason said, "It makes me proud to know I make you proud. You know I wouldn't be the man I am if it weren't for you and mom." Uncle Richard picked up Jason's bags and he said, "Man let's go ahead and get out of here. Your mother and that wife of yours have a big surprise waiting for you when you get home. Jason said, "That's the best ideal I've heard all day."

When they pulled up to Jason's three bedroom home in Flint. Jason could see an American flag flying from the garage that hadn't been there. Also there was a large yellow ribbon that had been tied around the big oak tree that needed a nice trim job. The next thing he noticed was a sharp champagne colored Cadillac STS parked where his Ford pick-up usually sat. There was also a Ford Expedition parked in front of the house. Jason said, "Who are all these people at my house?" His wife Lynn said, "Well you know my mom and dad wanted to see you and my brother brought his family over to welcome you home." Just as she finished speaking, Lynn's brother Shakim opened the front screen door, and their niece and nephew came running out. Before Jason could finish getting out of his uncle's truck

Rahmel and Joselle attached to him with hugs and joy that could only be expressed by kids. They said, "Welcome Home Uncle." Jason knelt down to give them better access. He gave them both a kiss and said, "Did ya'll miss me?" They said, "Yeah!" he said, "I missed ya'll too." Lynn grabbed her niece and nephew and said, "Ya'll let him get into the house so he can say hi to everybody."

As Jason walked into the house, Shakim said, "Good to see you Jason." His mother and father-in-law both embraced him and said, "Welcome back." Jason saw more balloons floating in the living room. As he approached the dinning area, he could see that the table was full of finger foods like celery, carrots, black olives and ranch dressing. There was also hot wings, chips, potato salad, and cake. In the stove his wife had held no punches on the main course. There was Cornish Hens, dressing and gravy, collard greens and corn bread. She had even made catfish because that was his favorite. Jason said, "Umh Umh! Somebody been getting down in here!" Lynn said, "We all helped baby, because I know you've been missing some home cooking." Jason said, "You know me better that I know myself. I can't wait to get some of that in my life." Lynn said, "You're going to get your chance. Everything isn't done just yet. Why don't you go put your things up so everybody can spend some time with you. He said, "Okay sugar." He gave her a kiss and went out to the truck to get his few bags. He laid most of the bags in the den before taking his personal's into his bedroom.

When he opened the door he saw his king size mattress with a lovely lavender spread on it. It was covered with rose petals some were even scattered over the floor. In the center of the bed was a gift box. He turned around to see his wife standing with a big grin right behind him. Jason asked, "What's all of this baby?" She hugged him around his waist and forced her tongue in his mouth with all of the passion that she couldn't show at the airport. After she finally withdrew – she said, "This is for the after party." At that moment Jason's heart skipped a beat.

Later on, after everyone had had enough to eat and the evening was beginning to wind down Jason's uncle sat down next to him and said, "You remember what we talked about. After you take some time for yourself and handle your business, I have a spot for you down at the plant." Jason was sipping his wine, "Yeah Unc, I'm definitely going to come down there and check it out." Uncle Richard said, "Ain't nothing to check out. If you want a job, come down there and see your uncle. I've been working there twenty-four years; I'll fire anyone of them slackers to give you a position." Jason just smiled he knew his uncle was felling the wine. They had R. Kelly playing in the background – *Step in the name of Love, Grove in the name of Love, Step in the name of Love ... ...*

Finally Shakim was like, "Hey sis, we're about to get out of here. The kids have to be ready for school in the morning." Lynn said, "It's okay, he ain't going no where. Ya'll can come by anytime." Her mom said, "Yeah honey, me and your Dad gotta be making our way home too." Lynn said, "Okay mom, I'm glad you all were able to make it." Her mom said, "You know we wouldn't miss this and Jason, I plan on seeing you in church Sunday." "Don't worry Miss Gladis," Jason said, "I'll be there." Then Jason mom asked, "Are you going to be able to help me to the car?" Jason said, "Momma you know you don't have to ask me that." Lynn gave Jason's mom a hug at the door and said, "Mom you need to let me know when you're cooking so we can come over. It's been awhile since I've been over." Miss Hephner said, "You know you can come over anytime." Lynn said, "Okay mom." Then went back into the house.

After Miss Hephner stepped into the truck, Jason was putting Uncle Richards take home plate in the back seat. His mom said, "You make sure that girl gets me my pots back. You know she has more of my pots and pans than I do." He said, "Okay momma," then gave her a kiss on the cheek. She continued, "And if you can find sometime, I need you to come help me cut my grass." Jason said, "I have all the time in the world momma, I will take care of the grass." Uncle Richard said, "You make sure you give me a call boy." Then he put his truck in reverse, turned on the headlights and was off into the night.

By now Jason was ready to settle down. He had had a long exhausting day. When he went back into the house he decided quickly that he would clean in the morning. He looked around and didn't see his wife in the kitchen. He yelled out, "Where are you at Sugar?" She yelled back, "I'm in the bedroom, come in here." As he reached the entrance to his bedroom, he seen that his wife had changed out of her dress. She had on a spaghetti strapped – see through night gown, that barley reached the middle of her rounded hips. It had white fur trim around the bottom of the gown. She was lighting candles on one of their night stands. She taunted him as her body parts shook under the gown when she walked past him to the other night stand. She said, "I hope you don't mind me opening your present." He glanced at the bed and notices the box was missing. He quickly looked back at his wife who was bending over lighting more candles. He noticed that she had no underwear. He said, "No sugar, I don't mind at all." He said, "Are you sure you didn't leave anything in the box?" She ignored his question, put a finger over his lips and told him to "shh." She began taking his clothes off carefully but quickly until she had gotten him down to nothing but his wedding ring and gold necklace. Then she dropped down in front of him and put what she could fit of his already erected dick into her mouth.

As she made circles around the head of his dick with her tongue, she could feel the anticipation he had through the heat and throbbing of his penis. She took a couple of more big gulps before standing up and grabbing him by his dick. She guided him to the bed, then laid him on his back. She quickly mounted him and guided his rod inside of her. She let out a sensual groan as it had been more than a year since she had had any penetration. She braced herself by holding his stomach and began a smooth steady motion of taking him inside of her, each time a little more. She did this for a very short while before throwing her head back and speeding up the pace until she exploded all over him.

She licked her lips, looked at him with a smile and returned to the first pace. Jason had been enjoying his self but now wanted to participate. He reached around to guide her by her hips but she completely stopped. Not saying a word, she gently grabbed him by the wrist and returned his hands to the side. With Jodeci – "Forever my Lady" blaring from stereo. She got herself back into position and continued the plan she had laid out for Jason until the sun began to rise.

# PART II

# AIN'T NOTHING GOING ON BUT THE RENT

After taking a few days to get things tight around his house and taking care of something's for his mom. Jason was getting bored with waiting around the house for his wife to get home. He decided today would be the day he would go find out exactly what his uncle was offering. During his morning exercise routine he was able to catch up on the news. The news woman was reporting that the police had identified six of the seven suspected bombers in Seattle. All of whom had died in the blast. They had been Saudi Arabian citizen who had some how illegally got into the country. They were looking for three more suspects who had helped in the planning. And were asking for the public's help. Jason decided he would check on his friend to see how he was settling in.

When Tim answered his phone he sounded tired. He said, "Hello." Jason said, "What's up my man? What have you been getting into?" Tim said, "Ah...What's up Jason. Man you don't even want to know." Jason said, "So you haven't went and checked into your school thing?" Tim said, "Not yet Playboy. My brother nem have a party on wheels going on 24 hours a day. It was hard to shake them niggas. But that is priority number one today. I'm also going down to the Small Business Association, to see how to qualify for a business loan." Jason said, "Yah – I am going to get on my mission today too. I'm going to see my uncle in a minute. But ay, have you seen the news?" Tim said, "No. Why what happened?" Jason said,

"They've identified those terrorist in Seattle, they said that they were from Saudi Arabia." Tim said, "That's fucked up. They should have just sent a nuke over there to kill all of them mutha-fuckas. Jason being the voice of reason said, "Yah, but all of them ain't like that." Tim said, "Yeah well, why spend all this money on weapons if you're not willing to use them." Jason said, "Your ass is crazy man. Make sure you give me a call so I can know how things worked out for you." Tim said, "For sure my nigga-one."

As Tim laid his phone back on the night stand, he rolled over and nudge Tonya on her back. He said, "Hey sweet thing, it's time to get moving around. I have some things I need to take care of today." She rose up and said, "Why can't I just wait here?" Mr. A.Z. said, "Na-Ann. I have to lock up. I'm going to be gone all day. I don't know when I'll be home. So I'll call you later." She jumped up with an attitude and said, "What ever then." And begin to put on her clothes. Mr. A.Z. had put on his pajama pants and house shoes and went to brush his teeth and wash his face. When he came out she was dressed but still showing attitude as she packed her night bag. He walked over to calm her down, he said. "I'll call you when I'm finished." She said I'm not trippen. Do what you need to do. I have some stuff I need to take care of too. So I might be busy." As he was walking her downstairs and to the door. He said, "Well I'm going to check anyway." At that she smiled. He gave her a kiss and watched her get into her car and drive away. He thought-unfuckin believable.

After showering and getting dressed in a dress shirt, slacks and a pair of Stacy Adams Outdoor shoes, he jumped into his Tahoe and headed to the community college. Once there he was told that he would have to meet with a counselor. He had a lot of questions for her. After he was satisfied, the counselor gave him a pamphlet on the Business Management course and an enrollment applications. She told him that he had to meet with an administrative assistant, and they'd instruct him from there. After waiting in the waiting area for awhile, Tim looked up an was immediately put into a state of shock. The woman who had come to help him was gorgeous beyond belief. She had golden-brown skin, long curly hair pulled into a pony tail. She didn't wear any make up and had a figure that would put the number eight to shame. As Tim stood up to meet her, she stuck her hand out and said, "Hi, I'm Fetiya." Tim said, "How do you do?" She said, "I'm good. I understand you are ready to sign up for a course here?" Tim said, "I am. My application is all filled out and I have my military discharge papers to help you process the loan papers."

Fetiya was impressed, she said, "Well sounds like you have it all together. Why don't you come into my office and we will go over everything." As she lead him to the office Tim was dazed by the shape of her round ass. When she stepped into her office she asked, "What course are you going to take?" He said, "Business Management." She said, "oh so you're a go getter huh? You wanna make that big paper?" Tim said, "I just know that I'll never get rich working for anybody else." She said, "That's interesting. Well you know you have to take and elective course with that to get a degree." He said, "Yeah I saw that. I don't know what I want to study though." Fetiya said, "Well I'm taking a foreign language as an elective. He said, "You're a student here?" She said, "Yes I have one more year before I get my Bachelors in engineering. I took Arabic as and elective because it's my first language, you know to make it a little easier on myself." Tim said, "Wow. It's crazy that you say that because I had to take Some Arabic classes in the service. I got pretty good at it too." She said, "That's good. You should further your studies, you never know when it might come in handy." Tim said, "You might be right. You and I could hold a conversation and no one would ever know what we're talking about. She said, "Yeah maybe." He said, "What nationality are you?" She said, "I'm Ethiopian, but I've lived in the states since I was five." He said, "Very interesting." She said, "Lets get these papers processed so we can get you signed up. The fall semester is going to be starting on Tuesday."

# C-LOC

It was late in the morning before C-Loc decided to get out of bed. He and Teflon had had a long night up at the casinos. Jackie had tried several times to pull him from the poker tables with no luck. What was supposed to be a night out with her man, turned out to be a night at the slot machines alone. While Clarence and Teflon (who popped up out of nowhere) got broke at the craps and poker tables. She was almost ready to head to her aunties hair saloon where she rented a booth. She had a lot of heads to do that day, but she wanted to make sure Clarence had breakfast. When he came out of her bedroom she had him scrambled eggs, and sausage and fried corn tortilla shells. He said, "What's happening baby?" Jackie said, "Nothing's happening. I have to get to the shop before I miss my client's." He said, "Your not going to eat breakfast with me?" She said, "No. We were supposed to spend time together last night. But I guess your card game and your homeboy were more important than me." He said, "You know it was not like that, I just hate when somebody is getting the best of me." She said, "How much did you give them last night?" "It was only about $1500," he said. But he knew it was closer to $2500. He said, "Why don't you reschedule your appointments and ride with me today?" She said, "Because I can't do that to my customers. And my auntie doesn't want her shop to get a reputation like that I have responsibilities." Well baby, it's not like you have to work there anyway. You know I give you anything you want. And I told you, you should start your own shop. She said, "Yeah well you say that but then you go and blow your money at the casino."

He said, "What does that have to do with anything?" He hated when she thought she knew his business. He said, "I will piss on that chump change that I spent last night." Jackie said, "I know," sarcastically. "You have all the money in the world, you can do anything you want." He said, "Okay. We're going to find you a space for your shop this week. Then I will be your boss, and I will cancel any appointment I want. And your responsibility will be to only me." She was putting on her saloon apron and grabbing the things she needs for the day. She told him, "I will believe it when I see it." He said, "I need you to take the truck today. I'm going to use your car." She knew he must have gotten a call from Mack, his only real customer. That was the only time he ever wanted to drive her Altima. She took the keys, gave him a kiss and said, "Be careful, I will call you when I am done." Then she walked out the door.

He was glad she had left, Mack had been blowing him up. He only did that when he was all the way out of work and needed to re-up badly. He dialed him up on the phone. He said, "What's up cousin?" Mack said, "Shit you know it ain't much dog. You know my girl is tripping and I wanted to go to the strip club to see if some of these bitches would scratch my bone." C-Loc said, "That's what's up. Where are you trying to go? Over to Centerfolds?" He said, "Yeah, why don't we meet there in about 3 hours." C-Loc said, "Alright cousin." He then went to his girls night stand where he kept his work and took out 3 of the 4 bricks that he kept on hand. He put them in a paper and plastic grocery bag and placed it in the front room closet so it would be ready to go.

After getting dressed he chirped to his brother, "What the business is A.Z.?" After a few seconds Tim chirped back, "What's up bro?" "Where you at, I need you to come ride with me" "I'm over here at the Small Business Association on Colfax." "Well meet me at the Soul cuts after your finished." Once Tim was through at the SBA he drove down to the barber shop. He thought ain't no way this nigga is going to get a cut today. He could see how full it was form the parking lot. He was leaning against his Tahoe drinking a Lipton tea when C-Loc pulled up. C-loc said, "You trying to be G.Q. smooth in that whack ass truck?" Tim said, "At least my shit is paid for." C-Loc said, "My shit is paid for too my nigg. Come ride with your baby bro." After locking up his truck, Tim hopped in with C-Loc, he asked, "What's going on Loccster; Your not getting your hair cut?" C-Loc said, "Nah man. I just wanted to meet here because you were in the area." He said, "What were you doing at the Small Business Association?" Tim said, "I was trying to find out exactly what I needed to do to get a business license and a loan. Pretty much they said I would have to already of had a business to get a loan. I was like how could I get a chance without help. She said to try other resources like a bank." C-Loc asked, "How much would it take to start your business?" Tim said, "I wanted to get and office space and a place to store some equipment that I would need. But I already know how to get contracts and all that shit. So all I need is about 20 G's. C-Loc said, "I have some bread that I'm going to open my girl a hair saloon with, but I have some loot I can loan you to help start your shit." Tim said, "Nigga your breaded up like that?" C-Loc said, "Man I told you I ain't out here playing with these mutha fuckas. I'm in it to win it Playboy!" he was pulling into the parking lot at Centerfolds.

Tim asked, "What are you doing here?" He said, "Do you remember that nigga Mack from Park Hill?" Tim said, "Yeah. We use to get work form that fool." C-Loc said, "Yeah well now he get's work from me." Tim said, "Nigga you have me riding with you to drop of some dope?" C-Loc said, "Damn nigga chill out. I'm just here to pick up some bread." He pulled up on the side of a grey Impala. As soon as he pulled up, Mack a swoll-ass red nigga jumped out dressed in all black Sean John gear. Then another dude, smaller but still swoll in black and red got out of the passenger side and folded his arms on the roof of the Impala. C-Loc and Mr. A.Z. got out of the car. C-Loc said, "What's up cousin?" Mack said, "You know dawg. Just trying to get it how I live he said, "What's up Mr. A.Z., I heard you was back on the block. It's good to see you made it back safe." Mr. A.Z. said, "Ah you know I ain't gonna give a mutha fucka an inch on me. Weather it in the town or in Iraq. Mack said, "I'm saying though what are you all dressed up for? You done went straight on a nigga?" Mr. A.Z. said, "Ay nah playboy. I just had some business to take care of. You know we can't be intimidating them fools when you go in their offices." C-Loc said, "I see your steady recruiting those youngsters." Mack said, "Yeah, that's my lil nigga Punch, he be putting it down in the booth. He's fixing to blow up, ya'll better look out for him." C-Loc said, "Yeah though let's make this happen before we get scoped by APD. Mack told Punch to come on over. He said, "Mr. A.Z. I'm glad your back. Maybe you can get your lil bro to give me a better deal." C-Loc said, "Shit man. I'm barely eating as it is. My girl said she's going to go sign up for food stamps to help out with the bills." Mack said, "Cut the games man, I know your family ain't hitting you like that." C-Loc said, "I don't know where you're getting your information from. But while you minding my business, go and try to see what another nigga will hit you for. Plus don't nobody have no shit like this." Mack said, "Alright man." Then Punch handed C-Loc a large CD case holder. Mack continued, "What time are you going to get that to me?" C-Loc said, "I got to hook up with these fools. I'll be able to bring it back by seven." Mack said, "That's cool, I'm going to be starting my bar-b-q about then. For Now – I'm gonna go in here and see what the latest fashion in G-strings is." Then him and Punch headed for the club.

Mr. A.Z. and C-Loc got back into Jackie's Altima then got back into traffic. C-Loc threw the CD case to his brother, he said, "Count that." Tim opened the book and saw nothing but stacks of $100 bills folded in half and wrapped in rubber bands. The placing for the C.D.'s had been cut away. Mr. A.Z. said, "Damn nigga how much was he supposed to give you?" C-Loc said, "It should be 48 Gee's." After moving some of the stacks around. Tim said, "I didn't count the individual stacks but there is 48 of them." C-Loc said, "Good." Mr. A.Z. said, "How much shit is he buying?" C-Loc said, "He picks up 3 keys at a time." Mr. A.Z. said, "And you have to take this to Pedro?" C-Loc said, "No, I already have the work. I just don't want him to know that." Mr. A.Z. said, "So nigga you mean to tell me that you just made damn near fifty Gee's?" C-Loc said, "Not exactly bro. It's like this, Pedro gives me 4 bricks at a time, for $12,500. So I owe him 50 grand. Well I hit these niggas for $16 grand a key and they pick up 3 of 'em every time faithfully. So that leaves me to pay $2,000 for the other brick. Or I save the other brick until their ready again and I pocket $11,000 off the top. After I look out for the homies, I still do alright." And every time I pay Pedro, he sends me 4 more. Just like clockwork. He was just getting off the highway on the Green Valley Ranch exit. He had Camron's-"Fuck Losing Weight" coming out of Jackie's 12 inch speakers. *Ay yo fuck losing weight. I'm back on these highways moving cake. Life's based upon what I'm do today. Buy a car or new estate.......*

Mr. A.Z. said, "What are you coming out here for?" C-Loc told him, "I have to drop this loot off at the crib. You know if I got caught with this paper, it would be almost as bad as getting caught with the work." He pulled up next to Teflon's 68 Impala in the driveway of their plushed 4 bedroom home. They both jumped out and walked into the house. They walked in to see Teflon and Static gambling on a game of Maddin. They also had the living room full of smoke. Teflon said, "What's poppin cousin?" C-Loc said, "What's happening playboy?" But he headed straight to his bedroom with the CD case. Static said, "What's up Mr. A.Z.? I thought you were coming back the other night?" Mr. A.Z. said, "Man I was going to, but if I hadn't of had Tonya with me. I wouldn't of even made home. Ain't no way I was going nowhere. Static said, "Well nigga I know your trying to quit. But you only have to hit this shit once and you'll be as high as the city." Mr. A.Z. said, "Nah nigga. I'm good." Static and Teflon laughed at him and continued to pass the blunt between the two of them.

Upstairs C-Loc was on the phone with Jackie and counting money. He told Jackie to call Pedro's wife and invite them over for Sunday night dinner. He knew by then his homies would already have moved the other brick. He also told her to keep her schedule open on Monday because they were going to get a saloon space in the Town for sure. After counting his money, he knew he was in a good place to make that happen. Once his money plan was all together and his safe was locked up, he headed back downstairs. He said, "Teflon I need you to come by the park later on so you can go see that nigga Mack." Teflon said, "Yeah that's cool, but he better make sure them buster's don't be trying to funk." C-Loc said, "Ain't gonna be no funk nigga, cause they know we have their work. I don't like fucken with them niggas either, it's just Matters of Business." Mr. A.Z. said, "Nigga we been cool with that nigga Mack since elementary. He even came to moms funeral." C-Loc said, "But still. You know ain't no love for the other side." Static said, "What are you going to be doing at the park?" C-Loc said, "My little dudes have practice today. We have a playoff game on Saturday, I think were going to get a championship this year." Static said, "Well I need to get some work from you, cause it's been popping over there on the U block. I had to fuck with this off brand nigga last night, cause your ass didn't answer the phone." C-Loc said, "Man I knew I should kept my ass out of them mountains last night. Nigga I got hit for 3 G's." Mr. A.Z. said, "Man ya'll better start making better decisions with ya'lls money." C-Loc said, "You already know what we talked about my nigg. But anyways I have to go drop this nigga off and then I've got practice. I should have that shit ready about eight." Teflon said, "You don't have time to get your head cracked on this Madden?" Shit it's only two o'clock." C-Loc asked Mr. A.Z. "Are you in a hurry my nigg?" Mr. A.Z. said, "Nah, I'm good. Do you have any beer in there?" C-Loc said, "You know I keep some brew nigga, help yourself."

# BE IN THA GAME

After dropping his brother off back at his truck. C-Loc swung back by his girls house to pick up the grocery bag that had the package. He headed straight to Aurora City Park where his team practiced at. By the time he got there the kids were already gathering with their parents. He loved this part of his life. To see the kids eager and excited about their dreams. They were still innocent, untainted by feelings of evil and greed that came from money and dope. He still remembered when he would line up against his friend Mack and he'd try to put him on his pockets every time. After he had given his team a pep talk about the upcoming game. The parents all went to the sidelines, and he began leading the boy's in stretching and running their exercises. It wasn't long before Teflon pulled up in his cocaine white Impala on 22 inch chrome hundred spoke Dayton's. He chirped into C-Loc "Wes West"? C-Loc chirped back "Wes Wit it"? He said, "Go ahead, the back door is open." Teflon Chirped back "alright. I'll get back at you later on."

# TEFLON

The parking lot was located at the back of the park, so no one noticed Teflon grab the grocery bag out of the champagne colored Altima. He was in and out of the park in two minutes. His plan was to go drop the package off and go spend some time with Dayna because she had been complaining. Just as he was going to make a right on 23rd and Fairfax the Denver PD was coming the other way and turned to get behind him. He said, "Ohh shit!" He turned his music down and tried to stay calm. He had his snub-nosed 357 up under his seat and that big ass package for Mack. He thought if these niggas try to trip, were going on a high speed. He only had to make it to 27th which was 3 blocks away. The cops had fallen back a little and he knew they were running his plates. He had a license and insurance but he knew the DPD were some hating mutha fuckers that would do anything to fuck up somebody's day. As he was pulling up to Mack's house there was all kinds of low riders and trucks on dubs parked out front. He swooped in as soon as he seen an open spot. He knew he was not in the clear yet though. Luckily, their was a few people hanging out side in the front of Mack's house.

He saw Mack's woman so he was getting out the car. He grabbed the case of beer he was going to take to Dayna's house and called to Macks woman. He said, "Hey baby come help me with these groceries." She came walking to the car and grabbed the bag just as the cops were pulling up. Teflon caught eyes with the officer and gave him an evil stare as he rolled slowly by. Mack had come to the front door just in time to see the exchange between Teflon and the cop. Teflon continued to play the role, he carried the 12 pack of beer toward the house. Teflon said, "Did you see that shit?" Mack said, "Yeah dawg, them muther fuckers been kind of thick you should post up for a minute." As much as Teflon couldn't stand the sight of a Park Hill nigga, especially wearing a lot of red, their gang colors. He knew he couldn't risk getting caught with that pistol. He already had a menacing and assault on his record. He couldn't take anymore felonies. Telfon said, "Ay yeah that's cool cousin. Shit - you want a beer?"

# BACK IN DETROIT

Jason walked into the manufacturing building of G.M in Lansing, just outside of Detroit. He had asked the receptionist to page his uncle Richard for their appointment. He wasn't really impressed with the appearance of the building. His uncle came in wearing some dark brown khaki pants and a button up dress shirt with the sleeves rolled up to his forearm. Uncle Richard said, "Hey son. I'm glad you made it. Your on time too." Jason said, "Come on now Unc, you know I'm going to at least be on time." Uncle Richard said, "Well don't just stand there and look pretty. Come on and let me show you around."

They walked through a door that led to a hallway that had pictures of American monuments hanging on the wall. On the right of the hallway was a huge break room. With microwaves, coffee and tea machines, vending machines and plenty of tables and chairs. On the other side of the hall were men and women locker rooms. They had complete bathrooms with showers. Also lockers where the employees could store their uniforms and clothes. Uncle Richard strolled past all of that. When they walked through yet another door they entered the main floor of the production plant. There were rolls of cars and trucks on the assembly line. They had hundreds of robot arms wielding and putting things in the cars.

Uncle Richard said, "This is one of the main parts of our production process. This is where the car frames get engines dropped in and connected. The vehicles whole electrical system is also hooked up and tested here before they move to other plants to get the interior done." He stopped at a rack and grabbed him and Jason a hard hat and eye protection. He gestured for Jason to follow him. He said over there is a dock area, we have products being delivered 24 hours a day." He said, "Now sometimes after the engine component has been hooked up, there are some technical problems. Your job would be to identify the problem and get it fixed. You also will be in charge of ordering all parts and components to fill the company's orders. I want to start you off as a quality control manager." Jason said, "Yeah that's tight uncle. That's right up my ally, I use to be a head mechanic in our mobile unit. I had to keep our Hummer's runnin you know?"

Uncle Richard said, "Yeah well – it ain't going to be that exciting. Come with me into my office. He led Jason to a secluded area back toward the break rooms. He had a nice office with expensive cherry wood furniture. And pictures of his family all around. He took a seat behind his desk and took off his hard hat and glasses. He said, "I know you got them skills boy. That's why I'm starting you off in management. If you stick around, the sky is the limit here. I have a lot of say in what goes on and I will put you where you need to be. You'll only be starting at $55,000 a year, but you'll move up quickly once you learn the ropes. How does that sound to you?"

Jason tried to contain his excitement, he said, "Yeah. I could make that work." He thought that's way better than what I was getting in the service. Uncle Richard said, "Well the job is yours if you want it. When would you be able to start?" Jason let all of his excitement out at that moment. He said, "I don't have anything else to do, I can start right now!" Uncle Richard said, "That's what I wanted to hear. We're gonna get you started on Monday so I can put you with somebody to show you around.

Lay Low had rushed home to get started working on a surprise for his wife. He was going give her the good news over a candle lit dinner. He had spoken to Tim in Denver and found out that his plans were coming together for him. He had said out loud to himself, "Man God is good." The house was spotless. The roast was in the oven marinating, and the home made mashed potatoes and green beans were done on the stove. He had a bottle of Red Mont a Chello wine on ice and he had some smooth jazz on the stereo. When Lynn walked in she didn't take notice of anything. She took her utility belt and threw it in the coat closet. She said, "Damn I get so tired of working with those people sometimes. I didn't get into law enforcement to make people's lives harder." Jason said, "What's wrong with you sugar?" She said, "This bad ass little boy had taken his dad's gun to school." She said, "They released him to his parents. But later on we got a call to the house for a domestic case. Well when we got there the father had whooped his little bad ass, like he should have. I wanted to leave it alone but my supervisor made me press charges." He said, "Sugar you can't let that bother you. You tried to do the right thing but it was out of your hands." She said, "I know but it can be so frustrating. I wish I would have been a probation officer or something, so I could help people more personally." Just then she noticed the candle on the table. And she could smell the food coming from the kitchen. She said, "What the hell do you have going on?" He said, "Well baby, everything ain't all bad. I got some news that will take all of that stress away." She said, "Well what is it?" Jason said, "I went down and talked to Unc today. Baby he's starting me off right away in a Management position and he wants me to start Monday." She said, "W-h-a-t. That's good. How much does it pay?" He said, "Don't worry about that. You just know that Daddy's back home."

Lynn wrapped her arms around her husbands neck. She said, "Yeah Daddy that does make me proud. But I need something else to make this stress go away". Jason leaned in and gave her a kiss. She rubbed her hands down the length of his body and took him by the hand. As she led the way to the room, he was being intoxicated by the sight of her ass in her uniform pants shifting back and forth. She kicked off her shoes as she entered the room and said, "And you know just what I need." She pulled her pants down revealing some sexy lace panties. But Jason wasn't waiting, he was peeling his clothes away as fast as he could. Lynn then pulled her panties to her ankles and kicked them to the side. She climbed on to the bed on all fours, but stayed close enough to the edge so Jason could get to her.

Not letting a moment go to waste. Jason placed the head of his erection into her warm, wet receiving pussy. He slowly pressed further into her canal until she let out a moan. She slowly started to move back and forth, which gave Jason a view that he could never get enough of. He took his hand and palmed her left and right cheeks and began squeezing as if he could release her frustrations from there. He loved the way she put that arch in her back to let him get to everything he needed to. He moved his hands to grab her by the waist and began to pound away as if he would win a medal. He continued having his way with her until she couldn't take it anymore. She relaxed her body, releasing him so she could lay flat on her stomach. But Jason would have no part of it. He turned her on her back and practically ripped her off shirt. He then placed his still erect dick back into her. This was a Jason that she hadn't seen in a while. He was hammering away deep into her pelvis. He was sucking practically biting her on her neck. And making groans like a wild dog after it's prey. It turned her on to the fullest. And just as she reached her climax, he got even more intense until she could fill his warm juices shoot into her. After that, he just collapsed and lay still on top of her. She rubbed him on the back of his head and she knew her daddy was home.

# ON DOWN THE LINE

Things were working out exceptionally well for Mr. A.Z. his brother had made good on his promise for the loan. He had shopped around and got some deals on most of the tools he needed. He was still trying to find a good deal on a van that he would put his company name on. His brother Clarence had even gotten a good deal on a spot across from the Aurora Mall for his girl Jackie. Tim was able to help him out by taking care of most of the minor maintenance and building improvements. That saved C-Loc some money that he was able to feed his gambling habit with. By night he had been very active with school. Turns out Fitiya was the Assistant in his foreign language class, and he had convinced her to give him some extra toutring. Which lead to a couple of dates and he had gotten very intrigued with her personality. He had finally made it out to his brothers house after he had taken care of what he could for the day. They were smoking weed and playing dominos. C-Loc said, "What's poppin cousin?" Mr. A.Z. said, "Nothing my nigg. What ya'll getting into?" C-Loc said, "Shit – I don't know its Friday, it's early. What do you have going on?" Mr. A.Z. said, "To tell the truth man I came over here to talk to you Teflon." Teflon said, "What it is?" I need to borrow your bike cousin." He said, "What, you trying to stunt for that broad?" Mr. A.Z. said, "Yeah my nigg. She ain't never been on a bike and I'm trying to show her some new things." Teflon said, "Yeah-it's all good Playboy. But you know Tonya has been looking for you." Mr. A.Z. said, "Man I ain't thinking about that broad. I'm really digging this chic Fetiya, I think she might be the one." Teflon said, "Yeah

55

she could be the one, Tonya could be the two.... "And Shayla can be the three," C-Loc jumped in before they all started laughing. Mr. A.Z. said, "for real though. Are you going to let me get it?" "Yeah nigga, here." He tossed him the keys. He said, "Make sure you don't dump my shit."

After swinging by his house to change gear, he came coasting up in front of Fetiya's apartments. She lived in west Aurora, in the hood not to far from one of his peoples dope houses. Before he could pull off his helmet, he was approached by a crack head. He said, "I'm glad to see you! It's checking right now baby boy. Plug me with something on a hundred." Tim took off his helmet and said, "I don't think I'm who your looking for." The crack head looked at him crazy. He said, "You don't have no work?" Tim said, "Nope." He said, "Shit." Then continued on his way. Tim got on his phone and called into Fetiya. I'm outside, I hope your ready to go," he told her. She said, "I'm coming out right now." After she had gotten near him, he said, "Damn baby! How the hell did you fit in them jeans?" She said, "Shut up? And tried not to let him see her blush. She said, "Where are you trying to take me?" He said, "I'll take you to the moon if you let me." She said, "What the hell is on the moon?" He said, "It'll be just me and you," and he got lost in her eyes for a moment. The he said, "For real though, I have this spot in the mountains. I think you will like it. Here, put this on." She said, "I hope you know how to drive this thing." And jumped on the back. He said, "It's all good ma." He revved the gas a little, then pulled off. He hit a couple of corners then headed west up into the mountains.

After they had gotton to their destination. The sun was just starting to drop behind the other side of the mountains. That spot he had chosen gave them an excellent view of the city. All of the city lights were on. Fetiya took off the helmet an stepped off the bike, she said, "Wow this is really nice. How did you find this spot?" Tim said "my mom use to like to have cookouts up here sometimes. On our way back down, sometimes she would stop here and just let us hang out for awhile." She said again, "Yeah this is really beautiful. I haven't never seen this many stars in the sky." Tim was showing off now he said, "You can't see them when your under all the city lights. You have to come up here to really appreciate God's creation. Fetiya looked at him with curiosity. She said, "I thought you were Mr. O.G., what do you know about God?" Tim answered, "I know a lot about God. He has helped me make it through a lot." She said, "Yeah well there's a difference between knowing God and knowing if he knows you. Have you ever been baptized?' He said, "I got baptized when I was a kid, but I don't really go to church anymore." She said, "Well you should. And you should get baptized as an adult. It makes a big difference." Tim said, "Yeah-maybe. But I ain't really trying to get on that right now." He grabbed her on the small of her back. He said, "Let's just chill for a while." She smiled and gave him a kiss on the cheek.

Once they had hung out long enough, they decided to make it back to town. Tim had pulled up in front of his condo and turned off the bike. Fetiya asked him, "What are you doing here." He said, "I thought you would come and hang out with me for tonight." She said, "Nigga your game is tight but not that tight." Tim said, "I'm not even coming at you like that. I just really enjoy your company and I would love if we could hang out a little longer." She said, "Alright-but if you try some shit I'm gonna bounce out of here so quick, your going to think you just got ripped by Carmelo." With that Tim just laughed. He opened his door and let her in. He turned on his lights and she sat on the couch. He said, "I have some left over chicken I was about to eat do you want some?" She said, "Yeah that's cool. She was grabbing the remote and turned on the TV. She turned straight to the evening news. She said, "Oh you cook too?" He said, "If I don't cook whose going to cook for me?" The news lady was saying something about, "up to about 20 suspected terrorist had been arrested trying to cross the Mexican border through Juraz." Fetiya said, "Come look at this!" Tim had heard most of it and was already coming to listen. He said, "What the fuck."

The news caster went on to say that they had been caught in three different service trucks posing as utility workers. She said, "That several automatic rifles, grenades launchers and explosive components used in powerful bombs were confiscated." Tim said, "Damn them fools were about to put in some work. It's a good thing they caught them." Fetiya said, "Yeah, that's a dangerous situation with them willing to die and all. I would hate for them to come across my path." Yeah I don't even want to think about something like that right now." Tim said. He was sipping on a MGD eating his leftover chicken. He said, "What else is on?" She started flipping through the channel and came across a re-run of the "Jamie Fox Show", she said, "Oh this use to be my favorite." He said, "Yah this nigga is crazy as hell." They watched TV. until late into the evening.

# THICK LIKE BLOOD

It was Monday morning and Jason was beginning his shift. He had gotten into a routine as far as the day to day operations. He would go into his office check on what deliveries would be made today and see if there were any new damage reports to take care of. He also had gotten into a habit of trying to shake Justin, the little Vietnamese that was training him. So as Jason was trying to have his morning cup of coffee, Justin came in to tell him of the daily agenda. As usual he made things seem more urgent then they were. Justin said, "We have lot's of supply come in overnight. We need to take inventory and get invoices on everything." Jason wasn't ready for all this so he told Justin that he would go check on the production line and see how many change order there were. Then he'd meet with Justin on the dock.

As Justin made his way to the dock, he was going over his reasons why he was starting to resent Jason. To him, Jason was a typical American who didn't know how good he had it. He had basically walked into a position that had taking Justin almost 10 years to get to. With only little more than a month gone by, he was already becoming lazy. He started going over the crates and boxes in the receiving area, checking them against the invoices. He heard a truck pulling up to one of the open docks. He thought something was strange about that, because their were no deliveries scheduled until after lunch. So once the driver had made it through the door and was going to open the truck door to unload his cargo. Justin approached him to see what it was. Justin asked the driver, "Excuse me. I don't...." The man pulled out a semi-automatic hand gun before he could finish. Justin dropped his clipboard and turned to run. Before he could make it anywhere, the back of his head was blown wide open from two slugs as the driver chased him down.

A couple of the factory workers heard the gun fire over the machinery and turned to see what was going on. There was the driver bent over and open the door to his truck. As the door opened several men dressed in all black including ski-masks came rushing into the factory. Each one posessed a military style machine gun. Some of them were wearing vest that had some exposed wiring and what appeared to be sticks of dynamite. As they moved past the dock and through the factory with military style tactics and precision. They systematically executed everyone in their paths. One employee had hid behind a tool box near the production line. But the troopers were moving very methodically through the factory. When he looked up for a chance to run, his face was cracked open by 3 rounds from a 9mm Uzi. There was pools of blood everywhere. Gun shot victims lay dying behind car shells and computer systems. Some people had found hiding spaces in the storage area and beneath furniture in some offices.

Jason was at the rear of the factory when he heard the first gun shots. He went into a controlled panic after the firing continued. He was moving with a lot of caution toward the source of the gun shots, when a woman-one of his employees came at him, beet red in the face and gasping for air. She said, "Please help me," then collapsed in his arms. That's when he noticed that she was losing a lot of blood from two gun shots wounds in her back. He knew she needed help immediately. His combat training came back to him all at once. He scooped her up underneath her arm pits and began to evacuate her back the way he had come. Giving up his plan, whatever it was going to be after he had located the source of the gun shots. He carried her through the break area and front offices that he had come to on his first day. Once out side there was a small group of people who had escaped some with minor wounds, helping each other. The unarmed company security officers had pulled up and was trying to get police dispatched to the scene.

All at once Jason worst fear was realized. Although he hadn't seen his uncle that morning, he knew his uncle was inside. He was always bragging about not missing work. One of the security guards helped him get the woman to what they felt was relative safety. He told the security guard that he was going back in for his uncle and turned to run back in. The security guard grabbed him by the waist and said, "I can't let you do that." Jason was enraged at the security guards actions and he was already pumping full of adrenaline. All at once he placed the guard in a head lock and grabbed him on his wrist to force him to release he said, "I advise you to let me go." But then two of the masked gunmen came to what was the greeting area and started firing indiscriminately into the crowds. Jason and the guard ducked behind the concrete walls that housed the big dumpsters. On the inside, Uncle Richard had been in his upstairs office when the siege of the factory began. He had heard an unfamiliar noise from downstairs that had gotten his attention. As he headed downstairs to investigate what he thought sounded like gunfire was intensifying. Once he made it to the factory floor and was going to enter the factory, he saw ski masked troupers yelling back and forth at each other. He had never seen anything like this and didn't know what to think. They were talking in a language he didn't recognize either. The cracked door caught the attention of one of the gunmen and he let off a round of bullets in that direction. Uncle Richard turned to run back upstairs but the assassin was right on him. He hit him with four rounds in the back before he collapsed on the stairway. Another gunman approached Uncle Richards's killer and said in Arabic, "no one is to make it through these doors." The other gun men were also screaming back and forth to each other in the factory.

The police were arriving on the scene by now but they were held off by the two gun men. They were able to supress some of their fire power and allow some of the factory workers to get further away. They didn't know what they had on their hands but feared it was another terriost attack like the one on the Microsoft factory in Seattle. A SWAT team was being assembled for an assault on the building to rescue any remaining employees. The FBI hostage negotiator were also in route to the GM factory. Jason's wife Lynn had been on patrol when she had heard the emergency request for all available law enforcement and medical personal come over the radio. After learning that is was to the General Motors factory in Lansing where her husband worked, she responded to this call with more vigor then ever before. Although she was on duty and used her patrol car to get more access to the scene than the on lookers. She had let all protocol procedures out the door. She was only concerned with finding her husband. She finally got him to answer her phone calls and he let her know where he was. When she finally found him, he was still creating a problem for some officers who were trying to contain him.

She said, "Baby it's okay, it's okay." Tim said, "I need to get my uncle out of there!" She said, "Honey there is nothing you can do. Let them take care of it." All of a sudden there was a tremendous explosion coming from the building that Jason was trying so hard to get to. Everyone ducked and tried to escape the flying debris. Half of the building had caved in on itself. The emergency personal was forcing people further back. Jason let out a flood of tears as his wife tried to comfort him. He knew his uncle was gone.

Mr. A.Z. had been out all day following some leads he had gotten off of the computer. He was finally able to make a deal on a Chevy custom van that didn't have too many miles and was in pretty good condition. He was now on his way to class. His plan was to get Fetiya to ride with him so she could drive his truck when he picked up the van. He couldn't believe that everything was coming along so well. After class was over he was going to take Fetiya out to celebrate. But once he got to the school their was not many people there. And the doors were locked with a sign hanging on them saying classes had been cancelled. He called Fetiya to see if she knew what was going on. When she picked up he said, "What's going on, why did they cancel class?" She said, "I didn't know they cancelled class. But a lot of places are closed today because of that attack in Detroit." Tim said, "What are you talking about?" She said, "You haven't heard what's been going on?" She said, "They attacked us again at some factory in Detroit." Tim couldn't believe what he was hearing. He said, "Who?' She said she didn't know for sure but it probably was the same people who had did a similar attack in Seattle. Tim told her that he needed to meet her at her house. She agreed and told him she'd be there in twenty minutes.

After hanging up with Fetiya, Tim tried frantically to reach Lay Low. He dialed his number three times before he decided to leave a message. He said, "Ay what's going on Playboy? I just heard what happened out there, I need you to hit me up and let me know you're alright." From the activity going on in the hood, you would have thought that it was just another ordinary day. What Tim had found out from the radio was it was in fact an attack on the General Motors factory. What he didn't know was if it was the factory where Lay Low worked. He tried Jason's number one more time just as Fetiya was pulling up. He had to leave another message. As she walked up to him she asked if he was okay. He said, "I'm good. I just can't get a hold of my partner in Detroit to make sure he's alright." She said, "Let's go inside baby. I'm sure he's alright." Although she lived in the hood, Fetiya had a nice apartment. She was a bachellorette and had a nice sense of style. As soon as Tim sat down she turned on the news and handed him the remote. The news was covering all the angles of the story. The death toll so far had been at 58 dead or missing and 26 wounded by gunshots or the explosion. Terror suspects were injured but survived the blast and were being held under tight security. Also, the terror alert had been raised to its highest level possible for the first time since it had been created. The director of Homeland Security was taking questions but not really giving any answers. The only thing new he added was they had received a video taped recording with someone claiming responsibility. Tim said, "I don't believe this shit." Fetiya didn't know what to say. She had never seen him upset like this before. She sat on the couch next to him and tried to help calm him down.

The news was beginning to play the video taped confession. It had a man wearing a ski mask and he was speaking in Arabic, but it was translated at the bottom of the screen. He said, "We are Al Qaeda Resistance Jihad of America. We are attacking your country in response to your attempt to conquer our Homelands. By your **indiscriminative** murders of innocent civilians who's only fault is being of the Islamic faith. But **now** you to will feel the pain of blood shed in your country." He said, "You cannot stop us, we are here. We will destroy your ability to finance the slaughter of innocent Muslim. Until you completely withdraw your forces from the Middle East, we will continue to destroy your economical institutions. The news lady came back on and said. "That – That was all that had been released and they will continue to bring more information." Tim said, "This shit is crazy." He tried again to reach Jason. This time – he answered. He said, "Damn man, what the hell's going on?" Jason said, "They killed my uncle man." Tim said, "Ah shit. I'm sorry to hear that homeboy. You weren't around that shit were you?" Jason said, "Yeah man they tried to kill me too. I just barely made it out of there. But check this out man, I'm still talking to the investigators. I call you later on." Tim said, "I'm glad you're okay. I'll say a prayer for your uncle. Make sure you let know me if you need anything." Jason said, "I'll be in touch."

Fetiya had walked into the kitchen to get Tim something to drink. When she came back he was off of the phone. She asked, "Is your friend okay?" He said, "Yes, but that shit did happen at his job. And his uncle died in the attack. She said, "I'm sorry to hear that. That's so sad." Tim hadn't taken much notice of her with all of the excitement going on. But once he got a glimpse of her golden breast reveled in her low cut blouse, he immediately started to grow in his pants. He set his glass down on the coffee table and said, "I didn't mean to upset you." She shook her head no, placed her finger on his lips and said, "Don't worry about it." Then she gave Tim a kiss that sent a cold chill through his body. Tim returned the favor with a kiss of own. He took her by the hand and led her to the room. Any other time he would have been all over her like he had just been released from prison. But she made him feel different. He controlled all of his passion – took his time and made sweet love to her.

# PART III

# "THOU SHALL NOT FEAR NO MAN"

After the funeral services for Uncle Richard, everyone gathered at Lynn and Jason's house for dinner. It was a very large turnout. From friends from the plant to strangers from the community showing up to show the family support. Almost everyone had brought a food dish or flowers. While Lynn and Jason's mom, Mrs. Hephner did there best to host the grievers, Jason and his brother in law had found a place out back to drink. Shakim who was of the Muslim faith was being very careful not to offend Jason or his family. Jason said, "Man this shit just don't seem right. Somebody somewhere should have an ideal of what's going on around here." Shakim said, "Well you know there taking this situation very serious now. You know they've activated the Civil Defense Corp and the National Guard down along the Mexican border. They have all of those southern states under Martial law. Ain't nobody getting in here or out without them knowing." Jason said, "Well hell it doesn't do any good to trap em in here. You know they're ready and willing to die. They need to start arresting all these foreigners until they find out who is supposed to be here and who is not." Shakim said, "Speaking of that, man there is something that has really been buggin me that I think you should know." Jason said, "What's that?" Shakim said, "Man there has been some strange things going on at the Mosque. Strange people a lot of ill regulars. I didn't think anything of it until that attack happened." Jason said, "What do you mean ill regulars?" Shakim told him that there was a lot of foreigners attending daily prayer services all of a sudden. Muslims from Sudan, Afghanistan and other

Arab countries. And in one of his prayer session he had heard a group of them praising the Martyrs who had died for their Jihad. He went on to say that the guy continued to talk too much and said the Zionist had not seen anything yet. And in a couple of days someone would be coming to make the Americans sorry that they had ever interfered with Muslim affairs. Jason said, "and who is that supposed to be?' Shakim said, "That he didn't know. This guy seems to trust me and he really wanted me to be excited about it." Jason Asked, "Have you told anybody about this?" Shakim said, "No. You're the first person I've told. Do you think I should let somebody know?" Jason stopped for a second, and really tried to analyze what he had just heard. At this point he really didn't have much faith in law enforcement. And if there was anyway he could get to anyone who had had something to do with his uncle's death, he planned on doing it. He wasn't going to get the police involved and let his Uncles murderers walk away on immigration charges. He said, "No man. Don't tell anybody anything. Let me think about this and I'll get back to you right away."

It was barley in September and winter was already showing his presence in the Mile High City. The leaves on the trees were turning golden-red and falling. And on this particular day the over head clouds were relentlessly thick and gray. It was a chilly 43 degrees outside, but that didn't stop the Bronco fans from showing their support. Even though it was only a per-season game, nothing set the city on fire like when their division rivals the Oakland Raiders came to town. C-Loc was having a game day cook out at his house. He had spent a few hundred dollars on food and alcohol and was now out side getting his grill on, so he wouldn't miss any of the game.

All the honey's loved to come to the Cash Cliques parties. They knew that it wouldn't be any funk there because they kept a tight circle. And all the nigggs were some major factors who stayed about their paper. Anybody that had a man from the clique stayed laced in the tightest fashion and was pushing a tight car. In the living room, the 42" flat screen was turned to the game but nobody was watching the pre-game show. Jackie was busy watching the group of girls who had showed up with Static. She wanted to know why the light skinned girl with too little cloths was giving her man so much attention. Teflon who was already full of Petron was trying to play DJ. He was supposed to be helping cook, but all he did was make sure C-Loc didn't miss his turn on the blunt. Tonya and Dayna were just mean mugging the other woman and thought they all were some groupies. By the time Mr. A.Z. walked in, he had missed kick off and it was deep in the first quarter. Jackie was the first to greet him. She said, "Hi Tim. Your brother didn't think you were coming." He said, "Yeah I wasn't going to be able to make it, but I convinced my friend to come. By the way Jackie – this is Fetiya." They both shook hands and said, "Hi." Fetiya said, "Wow there's a lot of people here. Did we miss anything?" Jackie said, "It's just football. Everybody is just hanging out." Mr. A.Z. continued to make his way through the house introducing Fetiya to everyone. When he got to Tonya he got nervous. It had been awhile since he had stopped answering her calls and he didn't know how she would act. When he tried to shake her hand and ask how she was doing, she just curled her lips and looked him up and down.

Tim just brushed it off and made his way to the kitchen for a beer. He knew he would need one. Clarence came in with a pan full of hot meat wearing a bar-b-q stained apron. He said, "Damn my nigg! Is that your piece out there?? Mr. A.Z. said, "Man Yeah! What you know about that. I told you she was tight." C-Loc said, "I give you your props. You better stay close to her." Mr. A.Z. said, "Man she ain't going nowhere. I'm just worried about Tonya flipping out." C-Loc said, "Now you know why I didn't fuck with her. I've got to go flip these ribs over my nigg." Mr. A.Z. said, "Who do you think you are, Daddy Bruce?" He went back in the living room and sat on the arm of the chair that Fetiya had sat in. The Broncos had made the first touch down.

Static had finally got a chance to speak to C-Loc alone. He said, "What's goin on with this work cousin? I've been trying to get at you for the past two days." C-Loc said, "I know Playboy. I finally talked to my people, everything will be straight tomorrow, I can't do nothin until then." Static said, "Nigga make sure I'm the first nigga you holler at after you touch down." C-Loc said, "For sure my nigg."

It was just before halftime when Mr. A.Z.'s phone began to ring. After seeing it was Jason calling from Detroit he excused his self down the hallway to one of his brother's spare rooms. He said, "How is everything going for you Jason?" Jason said, "I'm holdin it together." He then proceeded to tell him about the information that his brother-in-law had given him. He also told Tim that he had planned to go into the Mosque and find out who was responsible for that attack. He didn't want to talk about anything else, but he really needed Tim to come to Detroit to watch his back. Mr. A.Z. said, "You feel that strongly about it, huh?" Jason said, "I haven't been able to sleep bro. I've got to do something about this shit with or without you." Just then Fetiya came in trying to see who he was talking to. Tim turned his back to her and continued his conversation. He said, "I gave you my word I'd be there if you needed me and I'm not going to go back on my word. So let me tie up some loose ends and I can be there in 2 days." Lay low said, "That's good." I'll let you know if something changes," and hung up. Fetiya said, "Are you having problems with another one of your bitches?" Tim said, "What are you talking about?" Fetiya said, "That bitch in the living room keeps bumping my chair when she walks by and I came in here and your whispering in the phone you'll be there in two days. I'm just wondering if your having problems controlling your hoes." Tim said, "Baby it ain't even like that. That was my partner that got caught up in that shit in Detroit. He needs me to help him out with something. And as for that dumb broad, don't even pay her no attention." Fetiya said, "Well you need to come out there and be with me. These are your friends and I don't want to be by myself." Tim was getting very frustrated, but he realized it wasn't her fault. He said, "You know what baby, your right. Let's go chill for a minute then we can leave." And they did just that.

# DON'T COUNT YOUR CHICKENS UNTIL THEY'RE UNWRAPPED

The next morning, C-Loc went over to Mr. A.Z. to see him off. He asked his brother, "So are you just going to the funeral and you'll be back or what?" Mr. A.Z. said, "They already had the funeral. He needs me to come down there for something else." C-Loc asked, "Like what?" Mr. A.Z. said, "I don't know exactly. But he made it clear that he really needed me, and I'm not going to leave him hangin." Fetiya said, "Yeah he's not even taking into consideration what he has going on here and I want to know why you feel it's necessary to take a gun if your not planning on doing anything?" He said, "I take my gun with me where ever I go. So you don't know what your talking about, it doesn't mean I'm about to get into anything. You don't know everything." She said, "Yeah I guess there's a lot of things I don't know. And I see you want to keep it that way." She got up grabbed her purse and headed for the door. Mr. A.Z. called out to her, he said, "Fetiya....Fetiya." But she didn't respond. She simply walked through the door and slammed it behind her.

C-Loc thought it was funny seeing his brother get checked. He said, "Wow. You've got a feisty one. You better hurry up and tame her," with a big grin on his face. Mr. A.Z. said, "Man she'll be alright. We've been going at it all night, I'm glad she's gone." C-Loc said, "So how long are you going to be gone?" He said, "Maybe 4 or 5 days. I'm sure Lay Low just wants to get some shit off of his chest. I'm going to need you to keep an eye on my place." C-Loc said, "That ain't no problem at all. You need to make sure you don't get into no shit out there. You're all I've got my nigg. And if something happens to you I'm going to come out there and murder everything moving. Including this so called Lay Low." Mr. A.Z. said, "Nah. I'll be alright. And soon as I get back, I'm going to start finding some contracts to get this business rollin." C-Loc said, "Yeah, that's what's up." Mr. A.Z. said, "Well I'm about to ride up out of here. It's going to be a long twelve hours." So after they had given each other a hug, they jumped in there trucks and headed separate ways.

C-Loc had told Mack that he would meet him for breakfast at Village Inn. He was running a little late but he knew Mack wasn't going anywhere because he was completely out of work. When he walked into the restaurant, he saw Mack with his girl, and twin daughters already eating at a booth. He grabbed a seat next to Mack and said, "What the business is?" Mack said, "It's slow motion Baby. Just trying to get my ladies something to eat. I would have ordered you something but I didn't know what you want." C-Loc said, "Oh – it's all gravy my nigg." He had set his eyes on that oh so familiar CD case. He said, "What's happening little ladies?" They didn't pay him any attention but the waitress had made her way back to the table. She said, "Can I get you anything today?" C-Loc said, "Yeah – I'll have your sausage and potato skillet, and a Pepsi." She said, "Okay." He told Mack that he should let his daughters be cheerleaders for his team next year. Mack said, "If anything – they're going to be on the team. Don't let their pretty faces foul ya." C-Loc said, "Is that right?" Mack said, "Yah – they be going at it. They be terrorizing them little scrubs in The Hill side." They continued talking until the waitress came back with their food. C-Loc ate as quickly as he could because he had to get to Jackie's Saloon to meet with Pedro.

C-Loc flipped his last package from Pedro to some of Static's people, to help cover some of the money he had invested into Jackie and Tim's businesses. Now he was going to use Mack's money to get his operation back on track. So after they had finished eating they all headed to the parking lot with C-Loc carrying the CD case. He said, "Somebody will be by your house around 6 o'clock to get that to you." Mack said, "Alright then homie, I'll be in touch." C-Loc jumped in his Navigator and rolled his windows down just enough to be seen. He had some smooth 'Donell Jones' playing as he headed east, further into Aurora to his ladies shop. The rental space they had got near the Aurora mall was pretty nice. She had got two of the stylist from her aunties shop to come work for her. Her friend Ariel did manicures and pedicures at one station. And the fag Jorge did hair cuts and shampoo on mostly senior clients at the other. Jackie had a booth for her cliental all the way at the back. For a shop new to the area they stayed pretty busy. When C-Loc walked in Ariel looked up from her client to say "Hi." Jorge who was always over dramatic about things, completely walked away from his client to come and shake C-Loc's hand. He said, "Hey Clarence." It made C-Loc sick to his stomach to even speak to the fagget, let alone touch him. But he shook his hand and headed straight to the back room which he had made into his office. He stopped and gave Jackie a kiss on the check and told her not to let anyone bother him except Pedro. Who should be there shortly.

He locked the door to the office and put his Glock .45 on his desk. Then he opened the CD case and began counting the neatly pressed hundred stacks. After counting and recounting he was satisfied that it was all there. And it couldn't have come at a better time either. After his investments, he was down to about seven thousand in cash. But with the saloons lease paid off for a year and Mr. A.Z. had everything he needed, everything that came in now would be profit. He was really proud of his self. He took out his stash of purple cush and a Swisher Sweet so he could fire up something with Pedro. He was still breaking down the nuggets when somebody knocked on the door. He put the CD case in a dresser drawer and his pistol in his front pocket. He opened the door to see Pedro standing there smiling. He was flossing a thick 14 karat gold link with the matching bracelet. He had on a Dallas Cowboy jersey with the matching hat to the back and some blue 501's with the white Nike Cortez.

He said, "Whats up homie?" C-Loc said, "Ay – it ain't nothing much cousin. I was just getting ready for you!" Pedro noticed the Swisher in C-Loc's hand and said, "What up esay? You got some fire or what homes." Pedro was originally from Chihuahua, Mexico. But he got his gangster style in California. C-Loc always thought it was funny seeing gangster's up in Greeley. C-Loc said, "Yah man. I was hoping you had time to smoke one with your boy." Pedro said, "It's all good esay. I just have to pick up something from the mall for my lady before I head back." So C-Loc finished rolling the blunt and grabbed the CD case. He told Pedro to follow him out back. He handed Pedro the case and said, "It's all there." Then he lit the blunt. Pedro said, "That's good Vato. Unfortunately, you're going to have to wait on me to bring the yaeyo. C-Loc gave him a puzzled look. Pedro hit the blunt and said, "With all of that shit going on in Texas, my people don't want to move anything." C-Loc said, "Are you fucking with me?" he was still looking puzzled, this was not something he anticipated. Pedro said, "No – those fucking terrorist has shit hot homes. The fucking Feds are everywhere. I wish I could talk to them, tell them let's make some money. Stop blowing shit up – it's fucking stupid ay." C-Loc didn't hear the last of what he was saying. He was trying to see exactly what kind of situation he had gotten his self into. He didn't want to let on that he had missed managed his money, so he kept the Mack situation to his self. He said, "So when do you think your going to be ready?" Pedro said, "Ay – give me a couple of days. I'll figure something out even if I have to go get it myself." He took one more hit of the blunt he said, "That's some good shit essay."

Pulling in to the Detroit city limits was a relief for Tim, although he had made good time he still had been in the car for over 10 hours. He had only had to call Jason once for better directions and now it was just after

11p.m. and he was starving. After pulling up to Jason house, he thought not to bad. It looks like this dude would live here. Jason had come to the door way while giving Tim specific instructions to the house. He came out and said, "Glad you finally made it, that ride wasn't too much for you was it." Tim said, "Man please, after all of them convoy's in the desert, you know that wasn't nothing for a vet. Jason said, "Hell you must have been the only car on the highways. I wasn't expecting you for another 3 hours or so." Tim said, "Yeah I only stopped for gas, I didn't even sit down and eat. But that shit done caught up to me. Man where can I get something to eat, right now?" Jason said, "It's your lucky night homeboy. My wife fixed a nice pork chop dinner. With home made mashed potatoes and some of her home grown green beans. I haven't really been eating, so there's plenty left." Tim said, "Well let's get it, cause I'm starving. Plus it's cold as fuck out here." Jason said, "It's all gravy baby. I just need you to ride with me on this one. My wife didn't know you were coming, so just say you wanted to come show your support. I don't want her knowing anything." Tim said, "Yeah man what ever. Is she going to trip if she sees me eating?" Jason said, "Man shut the fuck up. Come on in man."

After they were seated at the table and Jason gave Tim as much food as could fit on his plate. Lynn came in the kitchen in some sweat pants t-shirt and house shoes. She introduced herself to Tim as Jason's wife and asked if he had enough to eat. Tim responded by saying, "I have enough for now, but I'm not going to make any promises." Lynn laughed and said, "Yeah I've heard a lot about you. My husband has a lot of respect for you." Tim said, "I'm sure he exaggerated but I'll try not to let him down." Lynn said, "Well I'm not trying to be rude but I have to be up in a little bit. So I'm gone leave you boy's to yourselves." Jason said, "Yeah baby – you go get you some rest. We don't need you accidentally shooting no dogs." Lynn said, "Nice meeting you Tim." She leaned over and kissed Jason on the cheek. Tim got a glance of her round buttocks and thought to himself "Damn." After Lynn was gone Tim asked, "So what do you have planned?"

Jason told him again the information he had. He said Shakim was going to introduce them around the Mosque. He said, "I'm just going to ask a few questions and find out who planned that shit. Then I'm gone send his ass to Allah or Habeeb – whoever the fuck they pray too." Tim just shook his head. Then said, "All right man I trust you know what you're doing." Jason said, "Yeah homeboy. I have the guest room set up for you. You need to get some sleep because tomorrow we ride."

It was just after 8 the next morning when Jason stuck his head in the guest room. He yelled, "Wake your ass up man – do you think you're at the Holiday Inn or something." Tim wasn't feeling that shit, he had had a long trip and wanted to sleep late. He said, "Come in here I have somebody I want you to meet." When Tim came into the living room he saw Shakim sitting on the love seat drinking a cup of coffee. Although he had never met him before he could tell by the Kufi hat on his head and what looked like a dashiki shirt that it was him Shakim rose to his feet and extended his hand and said, "How do you do, I am Lynn's brother." Tim shook his hand and said, "What's up, you can call me Tim." The seriousness of the situation was starting to register with Tim. He hadn't considered the full implications of Jason plan until they were all three looking at each other in silence. He looked at this Shakim to try to see something in his character. You see he was bred in the streets and understood every letter in the 'G' code. And he knew Jason, before giving his life to the Lord and marring Lynn had been a high ranking member of the Black Gangsta Disciples. He had demonstrated his understanding of the code in some tough situation they had gottin into in the service. Now he wanted to know something about this dude. He said, "Man – clue me into something. What did you tell these mutha fuckas about who we are." Shakim said, "Very little. I just told'em that you guys were children of African immigrants and you guys were trying to get away from all of the harassment that's been going on in the Muslim community. There is a lot of people doing that right now they won't think it's strange." Tim then asked, "And what's going to happen to you after this shit goes down?" Jason quickly spoke up, "Man I'm just going to ask some questions." He hadn't told Shakim anything about his plan and he didn't want to until he was fully involved. Shakim stood up for his self. He said, "Hey man Richard was my family too. Jason you know I use to be deep out here in these streets and I never forget where I came from and you know retaliation is a must where we come from. I ain't new to this shit." Jason and Tim both were surprised by his comment. Tim was a little more at ease when he heard the emotion he had for Uncle Richard. Jason said, "Coo. When can you make this happen?" Shakim said, "The guy that's been running his mouth usually gets there right before 5 o'clock mass. We can find out what else he knows then. I brought both of ya'll some of my cloths so you don't stick out." Tim said, "Damn Jason. This nigga stay ready like you."

# SLIPPEN

Mack had finally decided to get up and get to moving around. He had tried to reach C-Loc all night but never got him to answer. Niggas had been blowing him up to get some work and he was getting more and more heated by the minute. He was just sitting down in the chair at the barber shop when Punch walked in. Mack said, "Damn dawg- what took you so long?" Punch said, "Nigga I told you I was at the Outtlet's. I had to go get some new gear since my dumb ass Baby Momma cut all my shit up." Mack had to think to remember the conversation. He said, "That's right." All he could think about was what the fuck was up with this fool not answering his calls. He said, "Ay dawg this mutha fucka C-Loc is trippen. That nigga picked up my money yesterday and still hasn't dropped off my shit. And this pussy won't answer my calls." Punch said, "is that right?" Mack said, "Yeah." Punch said, "That's crazy – because I was fucking with that bitch Tonya last night and she was talking them niggas business. We was on some thizz pills so I thought she was trippen." Mack said, "What did she say?" Punch said, "Some shit. Fuck them Cash Clique niggas – they ain't shit. That's why they about to fall off. Said she heard the nigga C-Loc talking to Teflon about how that shit in Texas is fucking up their connect. I thought she was just hating but she might know what she's talking about." Mack didn't respond to what he had just heard. He just tilted his head back so the barber could get under his neck. He thought – I've been dealing with this nigga for over a year and he ain't never acted like this.

When they walked into the Mosque which was in an old section of

Flint, Jason was almost dizzy from speaking to everyone who greeted him. With everyone in their Islamic garments and thick beards he really couldn't tell one from the other. What he really wanted to do was bring in Shakim's 12 gauge from his truck and just start laying fools down. But he knew he would have to be smarter about this situation. He wanted to get the guy who had been running his mouth to lead them to the person who was calling the shots behind the scene. He had his glock 17, Tim had a .40 caliber Smith & Wesson and Shakim was leading the way. That's when this guy Yousef approached Shakim. He said, "Peace to you my brother" and Shakim grabbed both of his hands and said "all praise to Allah". These are my two brothers in the faith that have come here to worship, they have been displaced from their own Mosque because of government harassment." Yousuf said, "The Americans have no shame. One day they will fill the wrath of Allah. In what way have they afflicted you." Jason answered with the story he had planned over the last few days. He said that they at their home Mosque had been in touch with some powerful men from Sudan. And that they had agreed to give them $500,000 to start a private school for children of the Muslim faith. He continued the story and told how the Treasury Department had stopped the money transfer. He said that they then put them on a terrorist watch list and they had been harassed ever since. He said in the Mosque, at work, or even at home they were harassed. Yousuf said, "I have heard so many similar stories. But now it was time for them to be harassed." He said, "That the will of Allah had made it possible that all of them would be brought to their knees. Although we have a temporary set back, nothing will stop the wrath of Allah." Shakim asked him what kind of set back had happened and was there anything they could do to help. He said, "That one of the key soldiers had been denied access into the country and now we have the hard wear but we're having difficulty finding someone with knowledge in the area. My associate is very angry right now." That's when Jason saw his opportunity to act. He said, "I may be exactly what you're looking for. One of the reasons the government finds me to be such a threat is because of my expertise in explosives. I have my Masters Degree in Engineering and run my own demolition company." After hearing this information Yousuf was consumed with excitement and disbelief. He took Jason by both of his hands and said, (God is Great). He said, "You must come to meet with our commander." Jason thought to his self Bingo! He tried to conceal his anticipation with his remark. He said, "What about our afternoon worship?" Yousuf said, "Yes after prayer of course."

C-Loc's phone had been ringing constantly since earlier in the day. He wasn't answering any blocked numbers, unrecognizable numbers, but most of all Mack's number. And now he had just got off the phone with Pedro only to find out that nothing had changed on his end. He had just left Teflon trying to come up with a plan to get the money. But all he kept saying was fuck that nigga Mack, he would erase him and that debt. When C-Loc told him they weren't going to do that, all he could come up with was hitting a lick. By now he was tiered of his phone blowing up. He turned down his music and answered for the first time. He said, "What's the dealio." As if everything was straight. Mack said, "What's the dealio?" Nigga you tell me, you answering the phone so I know you ain't in jail. Why haven't you sent that bitch to come see me?" C-Loc said, "Nigga you better watch your mutha fuckin tone. Ain't nothing about my homeboy no bitch. I understand your concern about the situation, but your gonna have to wait just like me." C-Loc hated talking to much on the phone. Mack knew not to talk on the phone too. He said, "You know what nigga I ain't even trippen, just bring me my C.D.'s back and will talk another day!" C-Loc said, "Man you know how this shit works. We haven't never had no problem before. When I get through burning'em I'll get them back to you. Alright? Alright." Then he hung up. He knew Mack wouldn't take that to well but he had to buy sometime.

No one knew where he lived out side of the Cash Clique, so he hoped he could play him to the left for a little while. Hopefully long enough for

Pedro to make shit happen. After collecting what people owed him he was up to about $12,000. Now he was on his way to Jackie's house to see what he had there. After checking in his stash spot at Jackie's he was up only fifteen hundred more. He thought this shit can't get no worse. Out of all the niggas he was feeding nobody was stepping up to the plate to help him out. And his brother who owed him the most money was gone getting another niggas back. He said, "Damn this is fucked up." He took out his box of Swisher's with the pre rolled blunts and fired one up. He just wanted to forget the whole situation for awhile. He also pour him a shot of Petron. After a few shots and the whole blunt C-Loc began to dose off on the couch. After what seemed like ten minutes, but was closer to two hours, C-Loc was awakened by keys opening the door. Jackie came in and was startled by the figure rising off of her couch. She said, "Whew! You scared me." C-Loc said, "It's just me baby. Who else would it be?" She said, "Nobody. I didn't see your truck outside, so I didn't think you were here." C-Loc said, "You didn't see my truck?" With a puzzled face running to the door. Sure enough there was an empty spot where he had left his Navigator. He knew all at once that Mack was behind it. That made him trip hard. Not because his truck was gone, but because somehow they knew where Jackie lived.

Tim was getting fed up with the drawn out prayer session. Even though he knew what he was there to do, in the back of his mind he wondered if he was being true to his lord. He also wasn't too convinced of Jason's plan. After everyone was finished praying. Yousuf quickly returned to them. He said, "I have spoken to our commander and he is very interested in hearing what you have to say. Arrangements have been made for a meeting right away. We must go now." Jason said, "Where do we have to go?" He said, "Not to far. I will tell you directions along the way." With that they all headed to Shakim's Excursion. Before getting in the truck, Yousuf spoke to two men in the parking lot. They were definitely foreigners and they were driving a Ford Taurus. From his flaying hands and body language, they could tell there was some type of dispute. When he got in the truck he didn't mention anything. Shakim asked if everything was alright. He said, "Everything is fine." He then began to give Jason turn by turn directions. Only giving the next turn once they had gotten to every corner. Jason took notice that the Ford Taurus was following behind them. At one point during the ride, Tim's phone rang and he went to answer it. But Yousuf quickly turned around in his seat and said, "I am sorry but you will have to refrain from answering that." Tim was about to check him but Jason gave him a look in the rear view mirror like – Not right now. Tim gave him a fake smile and said, "It is only my wife she is always checking up on me." Tim thought to himself, 'why the fuck doesn't he want me to answer the phone.' After a short drive they pulled into a Crystal Inn Hotel. The Ford Taurus parked near them. Yousuf said to them, "Come – I will introduce you to our leader. He is a great man, very strong in the faith. You will be please to meet him."

As they were walking down the hall toward the elevator, the two men from the Taurus were not too far behind. They all got on the elevator together. No one said anything. The two new men just stood with some stupid smiles on their faces. Yousuf lead the way once off on the third floor and the two men insistence of following made Jason's group uneasy. Tim himself thought they were being lead into an ambush. He slipped his hand under his shirt and took Back Back off safety. Yousuf then stop at room 309, pulled out the key – opened the door and went in. Tim followed closely behind him; just in case someone was waiting to ambush he could be used as a shield. But to their surprise no one was there. This made Tim even more uneasy. He looked at Shakim and Jason and then back to Yousuf. He said, "You're going to have to tell us what's going on." Yousuf said, "This is a necessary precaution for our Commander. You will come to recognize the honor that is being giving you today." Shakim said, "Well where is he?" Yousuf said, "Patience my friend. He will be joining us shortly. Then one of the men who followed them from the Mosque spoke to Yousuf in Arabic. Yousuf said, "For security reason, I must check you for weapons." Shakim quickly responded, "That is very offensive Yousuf. My friends are here to offer you help." Yousuf said, "It is very important to us. Our leader is far more important than I and we can not take any chances." Tim said, "Well I will let you know. There is no need to search me. I have a gun and no one is going to take it from me." Shakim thought to his self – Oh Shit. Yousuf said, "I do not understand." Thinking quickly Jason interrupted and said, "You have to realize the amount of threats that have been made on us. You know with the hostilities toward the faith these days it is necessary for us to protect ourselves." Yousuf said, "I see. But you are amongst brothers now and it is vital that you are unarmed for this meeting to proceed." Jason thought, he was very close to finding out who was responsible for all this chaos that had been going on. He also considered the fact that what ever these guys where up to next, they needed their help. He figured the immediate threat to them was low. He looked at Tim and said, "it's okay – we will be fine. We will listen to our 'Brothers' proposition and then we will leave from here." As he said that he removed his glock from under his shirt and handed it to the taller of the two men. Tim's heart sank. He couldn't believe what had just happened. For all they knew they might not leave that Motel alive. But all at once he was filled with faith. For some reason he felt Jason knew what he was doing. So he too handed over his precious Back Back. Yousuf said, "Everything is fine. If it is the will of Allah – you will remember this day for the rest of your lives. I will return shortly – but again I must remind you to refrain from using your phones." With that he and the taller guy left the room. Tim had no doubt that the other man was armed.

Tim asked the foreigner "How long will they be?" But he just smiled and shook his head. Tim took that to mean either he didn't speak English or he was pretending. But he didn't take any chances, they were all standing on one side of the room and he spoke loud enough so only they could hear. He said to Jason. "Nigga have you lost your mind? What if they come back in here and lay us all down?" Jason said, "Why would they do that? It's obvious they have something big going on and they think I can help. They wouldn't have brought us this far just to kill us." Tim said, "Well even if they didn't. What the fuck are we supposed to tell this mutha-fucka when he comes back?" Jason said, "We're just going to tell him what he wants to hear. Agree to whatever plan he has, and then we'll come back tonight and put two slugs in his ass. Or better yet I'm gonna shoot his ass four times in the back like they did my uncle. At least now we know where their at." That's when the door opened and Yousuf, followed by the taller guy came back in and stood to the right of the door. Only then did this mysterious leader enter and they shut the door behind him.

There was nothing to impressive about this guy. He couldn't be more then 5'9". He had on the traditional Muslim hat, a dress shirt and slacks. He also had on some wire framed glasses. Shakim lead the way in introducing themselves to show the rest of them the proper manner. He introduced his self as Hasni Bibi and said that he was from Saudi Arabia. He said to them that he understood they were immigrants from Sudan. Jason said, "From Sudan yes, but we have gotten most of our education in the USA and our parents made sure we were aware that we were not of this land." Hasani said, "They must be very wise people. It is so easy to be taken by the great Satan. How is it that you were able to make contacts in your home land?" Jason told him that his father had worked for the Sudanese Minister of Defense after coming to the states; he still held a position in that office and was in regular contact with his counter parts. He said, "We have a lot of family and friends in the Government there." Hasani said, "My friend Yousuf also informs me that you were willing to offer you services and allegiance to my cause. Can you tell me why?" Jason knew he was trying to test him, but he was as focused and convincing as ever. He said, "As you already know the American government **sized** assets that were rightfully given to us. On top of that they have imprisoned some of our associates for political reason only. And they now seek to do the same to us. But I do not plan on giving up without a fight." Hasani asked, "And you would be willing to give your life in your fight?" Jason said, "I was always taught to stand for what is right. Death is not something that I fear." Hasani said, "You must be very strong in your faith." He then looked around at the rest of the group. All standing around with a concerned look in their eyes. He then said, "I will give you a chance to join our Jihad. You will first be on a need to know basis. After you have proven yourselves worthy – you will come to know more of the grand scheme. When I say move, you move. There is nothing else. Can you handle this?" Jason said, "There doesn't seem to be a problem there." He said, "Good. Yousuf informed you that one of our soldiers was denied from entering the country – correct?" Jason said, "That is true." He said, "And it is true that you have knowledge in the area of explosives?" Jason said, "In my business, there is no room for mistakes. There is very little I do not know." Hasani said, "I hope that you are right. There is a very urgent matter that has to be taken care of in Chicago. We have fallin behind in our preparations due to the access being denied of one of our troopers. This is where you will help. You must all leave at once."

Jason was caught off guard by this. He tried as hard as he could to think of some reason to stall. He said, "I am unfamiliar with that area. I will need time to chart out a route." Hasani said, "There is no need. Yousuf has made the trip many times. You will go drop off our package and you will be back tomorrow evening. Shakim will stay here with me until we have conformation that the mission was a success." Tim tried to stall. He said, "But what about.... Hasani said, "No more debates. Our target will only be at this location for a short while. We can not miss our window of opportunity." Realizing that they had already played their hand and Hasani had them trumped. Jason accepted that he would have to come up with a plan 'B'. He asked, "Who is our target?" Hasani said, "The guest speaker at the Chicago Stock Exchange."

# KNOWING WHEN TO HOLD'EM

C-Loc had been blowing Mack's phone up. After being played to the left all day, he had Teflon come pick him up. Teflon said, "I'm saying though cousin. That nigga ain't that stupid. He know we wouldn't let no shit like that ride. C-Loc said, "It ain't no other possibilities. I no ain't nobody else crazy enough to try that shit. Plus I have this niggas money. Why wouldn't he be answering the phone?" Just as they were pulling into their driveway his phone rang. It was Mack. C-Loc answered, "What's up nigga?" Mack said, "You tell me." C-loc said, "Nigga I ain't fuckin playing with you. I know you have my truck." Mack said, "You better be lucky it was your truck and not you." C-Loc said, "how the fuck do you know where I live anyway?" Mack said, "I know more than you think I know. I know your having problems with your connect. And I know you have my money fucked up with them essay's. But the main thing I know is if you don't get me my bread, I know it's going to get real funky for you." C-loc was standing in his front yard. He said, "Mutha fucka-." The phone went dead. He said, "ain't this a bitch!" Teflon was leaning on his car. He had heard the whole conversation. "So it was them niggas" he asked. C-Loc said, "Nigga I already told you that. Damn! I don't know what the fuck I'm gone do." "What the fuck do you mean? I know where this nigga sleeps." C-Loc said, "nah I ain't gone do that. Not yet. I have to think this shit out." Teflon said, "Ain't nothing to think about. Nigga that's disrespect and it's only one way to handle that shit." C-Loc said, "chill out man. This is my bad business, and I don't want nobody getting hurt behind this shit. I gotta think this out." Teflon said, "Shit, You're a better man than me."

# TEFLON

After trying unsuccessfully through two blunts and a pint of Hennessy to convince C-Loc to go to war, Teflon had to get outta the house. He couldn't stand them Park Hill Niggas anyway. He wouldn't give a fuck about how many of them died. He didn't understand why his partner was giving them respect. But if C-Loc was going to let it ride, then that's what he had to do. He decided that he was going to go to the gambling shack on the west side of town. They always had big money games going on there and he needed to let off some steam. But first he needed another blunt stick.

As he pulled into the shopping mall he seen Mack's grey Impala. He said, "it has to be my lucky night." He grabbed his 357 from under the seat and put it on this lap. He grabbed his phone and chirped C-Loc. He said, "Nigga guess who I got slipping right now?" C-Loc chirped – "Who." "This nigga Mack, fucking with some bitch at the Good Times" "I'm about to put one of these hollow tips in this niggas head so he'll think before he tries some shit like that again." C-Loc said, "No nigga. Leave that nigga alone. I told you I'm gone handle this." He sucked his teeth and chirped "all right nigga." He was disgusted all over again. Hear this nigga was carrying a fuckin hamburger – slippen with a bitch. It don't get no better than this, he hit his switch to make his Impala pancake. Then he turned up his music until he got Mack's attention. He had Young Jeesy blasting *I do it for them niggas with the the them rocks. And them O.G. niggas with the the them blocks. Hey.....*when Mack locked eyes on him, he hit the switch to make the front of his car jump up. Like a dog at attention. *This is for them niggas from the bottom of the map. With a fifty round clip for the bottom of the strap. Hey....* then he taped another switch that made the rear of his car ease up slowly. He gave Mack a look like he had just seen him eat from a warm pile of shit. He eased his foot off the break and coasted off.

The sun had just set behind the mountains and the cold Autumn night had taken over the city. The thick grey clouds blocked any light from the moon or the stars. Teflon found a parking spot only two houses down from the gambling shack. After he had locked up his car and turned on the alarm, he headed for the front gate. He realized the effects of the Hennessey was catching up to him. The front door was open so you could see the old timers playing cards at the dinning room table. He still had to ring the doorbell because the screen was locked and they couldn't hear him knock over the music playing. A pretty young girl answers the door wearing a tight form fitting dress. You could tell how chilly it was from the imprint her nipples made through the dress. Teflon gave her a quick once over as he made his way to the kitchen where the stairs led to the basement. In the kitchen there was another young girl, who probably was just barely legal wearing nothing but some boy shorts and a sports bra was pouring drinks. This one smiled at him and stared at him with her bedroom eyes as if inviting him to converse. But he didn't pay her any attention. He just made his way down the stairs and wondered how much Beans old ass paid those young bitches. He knew they weren't sticking around for the way he fucked'em. He said to his self "These little bitches must be making a killing off these old ass tricks."

When he reached down stairs, it was just what he'd hoped for. A full house. There were two different card tables and a pool table that was used as a craps table. He said, "What's up" to Beans who was dealing at the poker table. He knew it would be awhile before he could get a spot there. So he casually moved over to the craps game to see who was hitting. It was some light skinned nigga. With long braids in a lot of blue that seemed to be winning. He had never seen that fool in the town before, but thought he must be some kind of Crip. Before he could get a side bet in another pretty broad wearing almost nothing asked him if he wanted a drink. He said, "Yeah baby, why don't you get me a glass of Hennessy." She looked him up and down then headed for the stairs. He couldn't hate on the old man, Beans kept the ho's around.

After finally being able to fade the dice, he wasn't really up or down. And he was getting bored quick. The crowd had changed. Some people left, some had come. He finally got a chance to sit at beans poker table. Besides beans, there was three other players. One older woman who could have been in her late 30's. One older dude which must have been almost as old as Beans. And then a swoll as nigga who looked like he had done five too many push ups. Beans said, "Where you been youngster. I thought you would have been back trying to take the rest of my money." Teflon said, "Ah man you know. I've been handling Town Business. I know you weren't going no where." Beans said, "Well I hope you've got a lot of money. I ain't forgot how you tried to break me last time." Teflon said, "It must have just been my lucky night. You know the sun shines on a dogs ass every once in awhile." The swoll nigga said, "You let this young nigga hit your old ass across the head Beans?" Beans said, "That boy come in here some nights taking everybody's money." Then the older guy said, "Well he can't come in here like that tonight, cause I'm gone send all of ya home broke." Beans asked, "What's your game?" Teflon said, "I don't care. What have ya'll been playing?" Beans said, "Ay you know we play Follow the Bitch here." Teflon said, "Well follow the Bitch then." The woman said, "The name of the game is follow the Queen. Ya'll need to watch ya'lls mouths." Beans said, "I can call her a low down, good for nothing lazy bitch if I damn well please." She said, "Just shut the hell up and deal the cards." The swoll nigga said, "Damn Beans. She was good for nothing and lazy?" Beans just smiled and continued to deal the cards. The swoll nigga said I had one of them bitches before." Teflon thought to his self, 'how retarded is this nigga.'

The game had carried on into the early hours of the morning. The pretty lady whose name had turned out to be Therresa had long since left. And the older man had just decided to count his losses and get home before he gambled away the title to his wife's car. So it had came down to Teflon and this swoll nigga who called himself sweat. The dealer was able to cover all bets. When it came to Sweat to name his game he named a game Teflon had never heard of before. So he explained it a couple of times. Teflon had put a lot of money on what he thought was a good hand. But it turned out not to be the winner. Sweat threw him a couple of chips as a good faith gesture. But Teflon told him to keep them for himself. He would probably need them. Sweat said, "Damn little nigg I'm just trying to show you some love." He said, "What's wrong with these young punks today Beans? I try to spread some love and this nigga slaps me in the face."

Teflon was getting tired of this niggas arrogance. He said, "I got your punk homie." Sweat said, "Ay! Now he wants to get sensitive too. What's your game. Teflon said, "We'll play follow the bitch." Before Sweat had changed the game he had almost broke him. If he could get him to go all in on this hand he would do just that, then he was going to raise up out of there. As Beans was dealing the cards, this nigga Sweat was going on about how things have changed. Before he and his niggas had went to the joint they were the ones who had got all of this started. He said they didn't make hustlers like them anymore. While he was running his mouth. Teflon had gotten him to do exactly what he wanted him to do. Go all in. Besides that, with his wild card he had one of the best hands in poker. After the last call Sweat laid out his hand. A straight flush to the Ace, he said, "fuck with it." Teflon had five Kings. He said, "Yeah – take that nigga." You could see all excitement leave Sweats body. He said damn, I should have known when you kept raising me." He said, "That's alright. I gotta be getting up out of here anyway. Why don't you throw me a little something little brother. You don't want me to leave out of her broker."

Teflon being the smart alike he is said, "Man you're going to have to handle that on your own. You say you're a hustler, this just ain't your thing. There is a million other ways to come up." He was separating his chips to cash out with Beans. All of a sudden his head exploded with pain. He was knocked out of his chair and the side of his head was bleeding. By the time he focused, all he could see was Sweat trying to move the chair that was separating them. In one motion he lifted his shirt and removed his .357 then pumped four Remington hollow tip slugs into Sweats body. Sweat was knocked backwards until his body came to rest on the other table and chairs. It was only then did Teflon noticed the brass knuckles wrapped around sweats fingers. He couldn't believe this shit. That mutha fucker had only lost about two or three hundred dollars. HE took a look at Beans who had ducked and covered his head from the gun shots. Then he took off up the stairs. In the kitchen, he ran past the girl in the boy shorts and the one who had been serving drinks. They were coming to see what had happened. It took everything he had to calm down to stop fumbling his keys and get in his car. He raised his car up off the ground and skirted off into the pre dawn morning.

Jason and Tim had been gone for a little while, along with Yousuf and the taller of the two foreigners. Shakim had been having what was on the surface a casual conversation. But really was an interrogation. They had been discussing different views about Islam and politics. Yosani had said that he couldn't understand why all black men didn't consider America its enemy. And how could they embrace a country that had in slaved their ancestors and continued to oppress them. He also said that there would be a day when Islam was the only faith. Shakim was really just abiding his time trying to figure out what to do next. Yosani was getting relaxed with him and at the same time becoming more arrogant in his conversation. He was beginning to discuss the plans and operations of their organization. Shakim was determined to make sure none of it succeeded. Hasani finally shut up when his phone began to ring. He felt no need to lower his voice because his whole conversation was in Arabic. After talking for only a short while, he hung up and than spoke to the short foreigner who had stayed behind. He then embraced the man and kissed him on both cheeks before the man left the room. Turning on the TV Yasani displayed a sinister smile. He said, "The Imperialist enemies of Islam will finally have what is theirs. And that is only death and destruction. Tomorrow the whole world will know the wrath of Allah."

At first Shakim didn't understand what he was talking about until he started to listen to the news caster. She said, "That President Obama had just landed in Chicago where he would be visiting with his family. And tomorrow he would be addressing the nation from the Chicago Stock Exchange about the economy." Shakim said with to much excitement, "Your target is the President?" Yasoni said, "Why not! This so called President is responsible for the deaths of thousands of innocent people. He to is only a man and should not be above the law." Shakim said, "But there is no way that they will be able to get close to him or that building with any explosives." Yosani said, "There is no need to get close. Your friends are carrying a radio active bomb that is capable of disinagrating anything within a five block radius." At that instance Shakim was gripped by fear through his whole body. Yosani continued, "Let us pray that they will live to continue the fight." He then raised both his arms to begin his prayer. Shakim took advantage of the situation and smashed Yasani's chin in with right hook. Yosani fell to the ground catching the corner of the coffee table with the back of his head. Shakim saw that he was knocked out cold. Not wasting anytime he snatched the sheet from the bed and hog tied Yosani. Then he put one of the chairs against the door to prevent the foreigner from returning. After securing the room he jumped on his phone to call for help.

Tim had become very frustrated by this situation. They had violated one of the most basic rules in combat. And that was never to separate from you firearm. He trusted that Jason had had a plan. But now they were being held hostage going to go blow up some innocent people. What was worse was the only weapon they had access to, was in the back of Shakims truck which he was following. They had decided that he would drive the van with the foreigner, while Jason and Yousuf lead the way in Shakims Excursion. Earlier, after they had just gotten out of the city and on to Interstate 90. Tim's passenger had placed a call. Tim in turn tried to call Jason to see what course of action they were going to take. But the foreigner interrupted his own call and reached for his weapon to insist that he not use the phone. Tim had had enough of this. At the very first opportunity he got he was going to put an end to it.

Jason was making sure to stay at a cruising speed. Besides Yousuf talking about how this moment would be remembered in history. All he kept saying was to slow down, that they did not want to get any attention from the police. He had already made up his mind. He knew they would have to get gas soon and that Tim's passenger was armed. Once they were pulled over, he would retrieve the 12 gauge from the back so they could get him disarmed. If he tried to put up a fight, that would be even better. Either way he felt he could justify killing them in self defense. Then somehow he'd have to rescue Shakim.

They had been driving all night and it was coming up on six in the morning. Tim was low on gas and would defiantly have to get off at the next exit. He pointed to the gas gauge and tried to communicate to his passenger that he have to call ahead so they could pull over. But the passenger waived for him to pull along side the truck. When Tim tried to switch lanes, he was almost side swiped by a Chevy Suburban. He honked his horn and swerved back into his lane. He screamed out, "You none driving mother fucker." That suburban seemed to be followed by a convoy of SUV's. He watched as the last one passed him, then he switched to the other lane. That's when he saw that last SUV slam on its brakes and cause Jason to rear end him in the Excursion. Then the other Suburbans came to a complete stop turning sideways to completely block the road. Tim was forced to jam on his brakes. He looked in his rear view mirror to see swarms of Federal agents rushing his friends truck with fully automatic assault riffles. He then turned his attention to the SUV's in front of him. Even more armed agents filed out of them shouting orders. He threw the van in park and raised his hands in the air.

To his surprise the foreigner turned in his seat and tried to get in the back of the van to the crate they were carrying. All Tim could see was muzzled flashes coming out of the agents guns and bullet holes appearing in the windshield. He couldn't hear anything. All of a sudden he was eight years old again on a picnic in the Rocky Mountains with his mom. Then he was fourteen on the football field with Clarence and Mack. Next he was in boot camp running miles through the woods. Finally he was on his couch, lying on top of Fetiya while she massaged his head. He only came back to reality when he was being ripped from the van by a SWAT member wearing a ski mask. He was thrown to the ground and put into handcuffs while being held at gun point. After being raised to his feet, he could see all of the chaos going on. He could also see Jason was alright but had suffered the same fate as him.

Two agents led him to the back of an unmarked Crown Victoria's with red and blue lights only visible from the rear. One of the agents started shouting at Tim. He said, "Do you know you boys are in a shit load of trouble?" Tim said, "Nah man. You don't understand! We're on your side. We were trying to prevent this shit from happening." The agent said, "No you don't understand. Do you know how many lives you put in danger with that cargo you're carrying?" He said, "You soldiers have bit off way more than you can chew." Then he slammed the door. As he listened to the police radio in the back of the car. Tim realized how big of a mistake they had made. Once again he made a request of God. He promised that if he would get him out of this mess that he would only do right from now on.

# C-LOC

It was barely coming on nine o'clock in the morning, but C-Loc had already been moving around for almost five hours. Teflon had shown up in the wee hours of the morning like he sometimes did. But this time he burst into C-Loc's room while he and Jackie were still asleep. Being startled out of his sleep was nothing compared to the situation he found his partner had gotten into. He practically had to cover Teflon's mouth with his hands to convince him to shut up in front of Jackie. After he had calmed his friend down and they had some privacy he was able to make since of what Teflon was saying. He also quickly realized that if what he had heard was true, then the police would be looking for a cocaine white Impala. So the first thing he did was to pull his Camaro out of the garage and put the Impala in its place. He also covered the car with a tarp. After Teflon had taken a shower to wash off any gun residue and changed clothes he bandaged up his head wound. They also took his dirty clothes and burned them in the fire place with two duro logs. But now he wanted to be sure that this guy was actually dead.

Since his truck was still gone, he had no choice but to use Jackie's Altima. The Camaro was to flashy and he couldn't risk being pulled over with this hot commodity, his friend in the car and on top of everything going on Jackie was worried about missing her appointments. She said, "Well how am I supposed to get to the shop?" He said, "You're going to have to take my car." "I don't want to drive your car and you know those guys are still looking for you," she said. He said, "Bitch then don't go to the shop today. Don't you see I have a serious situation going on here?" she said, "Well what are you getting mad at me for?" He said, "I don't have time for this shit. Either take the car or cancel your appointments. I don't give a fuck. I'll be back as soon as I can." Then he snatched the keys from the kitchen counter and he and Teflon bounced.

In the car he had Teflon go over the story again, then he asked if he was positive the nigga died. He said, "Remember them niggas hit the big homie five times close range." Teflon didn't respond. He had seen the mess those hollow tips had made and he wasn't even going to attempt to deceive himself with futile thinking. Teflon had been in a trance and didn't even notice how bold C-Loc was acting. Before he knew it, they were passing by the crime scene that not to long ago he had sped away from. Sure enough there was still a lot of police activity, but out of everything, it was the yellow tape that made Teflon burst into tears of regret. C-Loc didn't know what to say. He just told his friend that it wasn't as bad as it seemed and that things would work themselves out. He said, "shit you know that mutha fucka Beans ain't giving up no info. Teflon had no doubt in his mind about that. He was more concerned about the girls that were serving drinks and the other people there that knew he frequented the place. He knew it was only a matter of time before the Gang Unit found out who Teflon was.

He said, "Ay man. I need to go by my mom's house." C-Loc didn't agree with this but he was down with his homie one hundred percent. His mom had a house in south Denver which was only about a twenty minute drive. C-Loc advised him to be as discreet and quick as possible while in there. When he walked in, his mom was putting her lunch together for work. She said, "Hey James. What are you doing here?" I was just in the neighborhood, I wanted to say hi," he said as he walked over to give his mom a hug. He hugged his mom like he hadn't seen her in years then he gave her a kiss on the cheek. She said, "What's gotten into you? I know you ain't trying to ask us for more money." He said, "No ma. I just want you to know I love you and even though it doesn't seem like it, I do listen when you tell me stuff." She said, "What have you been crying for?" He said, "Oh – um me and Dayna got into a fight and I'm just tired of it." She said, "You and your hookers. I told you them girls ain't no good. You need to go to church so you can get you a good woman." "I know mom," he said. She said, "Well I have to go. I'm not going to have ya'll making me late." He said, "Okay mom. I'll lock the door before I leave." He gave his mom another hug and kiss before she left. After she was gone he went into his room down in the basement to his other safe and took all the money out. He took five thousand and put it in his mom's favorite cooking pot where she would be sure to find it. If anything happened to him it was the least he could do after all she had done for him.

Then he told C-Loc that he wanted to spend sometime with Dayna. Dayna had always been a good girl and when they showed up unannounced it was a pleasant surprise. She couldn't understand why James was being more affectionate than usual but still she was happy that he had finally showed up. After she gave him his weed tray that she knew he would be asking for, she went to fix them some breakfast. There wasn't much of a conversation over breakfast and when they were through Teflon told her that he needed to speak in private with C-Loc but he would be with her shortly. They discussed some of the options he felt he had and the one he favored the least was to hire a lawyer and turn himself in. After a couple of blunts he told his friend that he would stay put for now but to wait for him to contact him. C-Loc told him. "Don't trip. I have your back to the end. You ride for me-I ride for you. I still remember our deal."

# THE GINGER BREAD MAN

*Ain't no need for me to play the role like I was*
*superman. When they kick in tha door.*
*I was already on the floor sayin, "Please*
*don't shot me man!" X-Rated*

Later on that night Teflon received a disturbing phone call from his mother. She was crying and on the verge of a serious anxiety attack. She said, "James what is going on with you?" These people are at my house talking about you done shot somebody." He said, "don't believe'em momma. I haven't done nothing." She said, "Well they're all over the place talking about I need to convince you to talk to them. I told them I don't know where you could be." That was his cue to let him know that she had his back. She knew damn well where he was at. He said, "mom don't worry about it. I didn't do nothing and they can't prove I did anything." She said, "This man wants to talk to you." The man voice said, "Hey – James." Teflon said, "Yes." He said, "Ay man we just want to ask you a few questions. We don't want to get your mom involved with this. We just want to hear your side of the story. Can you come talk to us?" Teflon said, "I don't have anything to talk to ya'll about." The man said, "If you didn't do anything then you don't have anything to worry about. Is there anyway you can meet us here?" Teflon said, "I guess so. It ain't like ya'll are going to leave me alone." The man said, "We just want to know what happened." Teflon said, "I'll be there in twenty minutes." And after the phone was hung up he said, "you mutha fuckas better put out and APB. It'll be a cold day in hell before I walk into a police station. That night on the evening news James and his story was in the headlines.

# SENT FROM HEAVEN

*"Do what you gotta do. But know you gotta change."*
*"Try to find a way to make it out the game."*
**Tupac Shakur**

Jason felt like his stomach would burst behind the wheel of his wife's new Mercedes Benz. After Sunday services at church, he and his wife had went over his mom's house for dinner. It was one of the best spare rib dinners he had ever had. He could never get enough of his mom's cabbage, corn bread, and black eye peas with the bacon mixed in for more flavor. And even though Lynn was three months pregnant, he could tell that her stomach could not contain another bite. She leaned her head against the passenger window as they cruised down the highway. He was amazed at the way she glowed since they found out that she was pregnant. With her hair pulled back into a ponytail and no make up, she was more beautiful to him now then ever before. And since she had left the police department, they were able to make up for some of the lost times.

He could still remember that day back in September when she had come barging into that Federal holding center demanding to see her husband. Him and Tim were being brought in front of a judge to see if there was enough evidence to bring charges on them. She had showed up with one of the best lawyers from Detroit. And all though he was able to get them freed and clear of all charges, she was the real hero. After receiving a call from Shakim, her and her partner responded to the motel immediately. Then they took Yosani into custody for terrorist activity and attempting to assassinate the President. Upon hearing the details of the assassination plot and learning that her husband had been kidnapped. She called on of her connections in the FBI. They then contacted the On-Star service provider and were able to locate Shakims Excursion. A FBI counter-terrorism team was sent to intercept them before they reached the city. And even thought the other foreigner was never apprehended it turned out that Yosani was on the ten most wanted list and had a five hundred thousand dollar reward on his head. After splitting the reward with Tim and Shakim, he had made out with a little more that $165,000.

It made him proud to be able to give his wife a brand new Mercedes for Christmas. After all the drama had calmed down, he was able to return to work for GM. Out of all that he had been through, the hardest thing to believe was that he was going to be a father. Before he could get off the highway his phone rang. It was Tim. He said, "Tim – my nigga. What's up with you man?" Tim said, "Ay, I'm just trying to see if you wanted to do something on this Broncos and Lions game tonight." He said, "Nah, I don't want to take your money like that. Where are they playing at anyways?" Tim said, "They're out here. And as soon as I leave this jail, I'm headed down to the stadium.. I have some tight ass seats near the fifty yard line." Jason said, "They still haven't let your boy out of there?" He said, "Nope. He'll be going to court this week. We're just going to say what's up to him." Jason said, "Well call me at halftime. I want to see how my boys are acting before I put any money on them." Tim said, "You know I am too. Alright then, one."

Pulling into the Arapahoe County jail, C-Loc began to spray himself with cologne to cover the smell of weed he had been smoking. His brother had been able to make good on the money owed to Mack with some reward money he had gotten from fuckin with Lay Low. After he had gotten his Navigator back, him and Mack were cool enough to squash their funk. And that was a good thing because it was going on four months since the government had put a crack down on the borders. And Pedro's people were still unable to move anything.

Jackie's shop was still doing good and she had moved in with him so they could save even more money. He had also started to work as Tim assistant at his property maintenance company. He felt good not having to look over his shoulders – as much. As they were walking up to the visitors entrance Tim said, "Nigga I need you to open up the shop tomorrow morning. Fetiya has an interview and she doesn't know how to get there." C-Loc said, "Damn man. Every since she moved in with you she's been shortening your lease every chance she gets." Tim said, "Man you're worried about the wrong things. You just make sure you're there by seven."

They didn't have to wait long because their visit was set for 4:00p.m. Teflon came to the cubicle wearing that famous orange jump suit with his hair pulled into a ponytail. He sat down wearing a big grin and picked up the phone. He said, "What's popping cousin," putting his fist up to the screen for some dap. C-Loc said, "Ain't nothing cousin. You know its all day everyday trying to get a buck. Are you alright?" Teflon said, "Shit nigga, you know I'm alright. These niggas don't want no problems." C-Loc said, "Yeah I know that. I'm saying though, have you heard anything?" He said, "As a matter of fact I did. You know my moms and them got me a tight ass lawyer. He came and seen my yesterday. He said the DA was willing to drop the 'M' case if I plead to illegal possession of a hand gun by a felon with a maximum of five year sentence." C-Loc said. "Damn your lawyer got him to do all that?" he said, "Yeah – I told you that nigga was trying to rob me. Look at this scar upside my head." Then he turned his head to the side and pointed to it. C-Loc said, "Yeah I see. So are you gonna take it?" He said, "Hell yeah! I don't want to take nothing but you know the Feds could pick up that heat case and stretch my ass out. With this deal, I'll be out in twenty-four months. You know that ain't shit."

C-Loc said, "That's cool then cousin. You know you're my mutha fucka and you know I got you." Teflon said, "For sure my nigg."

Tim got on the phone and said, "What's good with you homie?" He said, "It ain't shit. Just something I gotta do. You know God ain't gone give me more that I can handle." Tim started laughing. He said, "Where did you hear that from?" Teflon said, "You ain't the only one that gets into those scriptures. You know I pray every now and then. I hear that broad is trying to get you to become a minister." Tim said, "It ain't all like that. I did get baptized at her church and I'm there every Sunday. But that's because of my own convictions." He said, "yeah well it's good to have that assurance." Tim said, "I'm going to leave five hundred dollars up here for your commissary. If you need anything else let me know." Teflon said, "That's what's up. But this visit is about to end so ya'll be careful." Tim said, "All ways," then the screen went blank.

They didn't say anything to each other walking back to the truck. Once they got in, C-Loc said, "Damn that nigga got lucky." As he was reaching into the ashtray for the blunt he had put out. He said, "Do you remember this." And he skipped through a few songs on the CD player. Tim said, "Do you have to light that shit up again?" C-Loc said, "This is my shit. If I was in your shit I wouldn't be telling you what to do. Just try not to inhale it." Then he turned up a song that had been an A-town classic *'So I'm about to hit the room, and get a Mile High. Cause I ain't Nathan Nice – We gone show these other fools, that they ain't doing shit unless they get a Mile High.....'*

# ABOUT THE AUTHOR

Bailiwick, barony, business, circle, discipline, domain, element, fiefdom, precinct, province, realm, terrain, and walk.

It's first thing in the morning. Rays of sunlight penetrate your eyelids, forcing you to wake from a deep slumber. Every creature, creation, and creator has an agenda for the day; including you. In your sleep, you dreamed of a place, or position in life. One where the elements that affect your thoughts daily, somehow meshed together peacefully. One where you can stand firm on what you believe in.

One where you speak with confidence - and intelligence about the subjects you choose to spend your breath on. You plan the things you will accomplish today. And they are accomplished. To some this is referred to as "being successful". To me, this is called a "Kingdom".

Lightning Source UK Ltd.
Milton Keynes UK
UKHW012019080621
385174UK00001B/8